HUNGER
AND OTHER STORIES

HUNGER
AND OTHER STORIES

Narendra Kohli

Translated from Hindi by

Rekha Gupta

FULL CIRCLE HPB

HUNGER AND OTHER STORIES

First Paperback Edition, 2009
ISBN 978-81-216-1371-2

Published by

Hind Pocket Books Pvt. Ltd.

J-40, Jorbagh Lane, New Delhi-110003
Tel: 24620063, 24621011 • Fax: 24645795
or Post Box No. 3005, Lodhi Road Post Office, New Delhi-110003
E-mail: fullcircle@vsnl.com • *website:* www.atfullcircle.com

Designing & Typesetting : SCANSET
J-40, Jorbagh Lane, New Delhi-110003

Printed at Dot Securities Press, New Delhi-110028

PRINTED IN INDIA

08/09/05/01/11/SCANSET/GS/DSP/DSP/NP250/NP250

THE STORIES

HUNGER

The two of them were cycling furiously in the dusk.

They startled any occasional passerby they met. Curious, the passerby would pause a moment to stare at the two, and then go his own way. Though they were not afraid of the odd person they passed, they would noticeably quicken their pace. They encountered neither looting nor burning, nor an armed mob. It was sheer chance that they had met no policemen, no army truck; after all, the camp wasn't all that close to Deputy Bagh.

They finally reached Trunkwala Bazaar. Their lane was scarcely more than twenty yards away. Suddenly, both slowed down. Gopal looked back at Birju and smiled.

The anxiety was washed off Birju's face. He even seemed to be quite confident but was still guarded.

"Don't ring the cycle bell, Gopal babu!" Birju whispered.

"Why?" Gopal raised his bushy eyebrows.

"What if someone is hiding around here?" said Birju, "you ring the bell and before you know it, he'll stick a knife in your guts in the dark."

"There's no one here." Gopal pushed the front wheel of his bike into the lane. "What's there to fear in our own lane?"

Suddenly, from Krishna Cottage, the first house in the lane, out jumped a strapping figure who stood before them and bellowed, "who's there?"

Both of them realised that this was no rioter. Standing at attention before them was a soldier holding a rifle … most probably a Baluch. Yes! It was a Baluch. The ruthless red face, long brownish hair, red cap and that thundering voice! It had to be a Baluch. So their area was also under army control!

"Who are you?" he demanded threateningly, picking up his gun.

"I'm Gopal and this is Birju," Gopal said pointlessly, swallowing the spit in his mouth. He looked intently at the soldier's face.

"Why have you come here?" the Baluch asked. Sensing their fear, he lowered his gun.

Gopal hesitated… no, he wouldn't kill them.

He wasn't some riff-raff. He was a disciplined, responsible soldier.

"We've come home. It's the fifth house in the lane," he answered, his voice steady now.

"If you wanted to return home, then why did you run away and abandon it in the first place?" laughed the Baluch.

"Yesterday the *musalmaans* attacked our *mohalla*. Two houses were set on fire. That's why we ran away," said Gopal.

"So what brings you here?" There was sarcasm rather than curiosity in his voice.

For a moment, Gopal stared at him fearfully. Then, looking down at the ground, he answered, "My mother is very sick. She can't sleep without some bedding. We've come to fetch her bedding."

The Baluch guffawed loudly. "Boys, your mother loves her bedding more than your lives. Suppose someone stabs you on the way…" he paused, …"or if I shoot you for ignoring the curfew. Then you'll sleep till eternity without any bedding at all!"

He was toying casually with the gun in his hand.

Both of them were stunned. Frozen, they stood motionless. The ease they had felt a moment ago was gone in an instant. A pool of foul liquid gathered in Birju's mouth. He did not know that his lower lip had sagged. He was weeping, "I'm only a servant. Gopal babu was coming to get his mother's bedding. Lalaji sent me along to pick up a few things."

"Servant!" The soldier lowered his gun. Abruptly, his tone changed. In a deep authoritative voice, he said, "all right! Go to your house. Stay quietly indoors all night. Don't lock the door from within, but don't come out either. Curfew is on now. If you're still alive in the morning, you can go back to the camp quietly when the curfew is lifted. And look, don't you try to carry any baggage with you. Go back and tell the fools who sent you that you will get shot if you go hauling things around."

Wheeling their cycles very slowly, the two of them moved on. Birju looked back over his shoulder lest the Baluch shoot them from behind the minute they turned. But nothing like that happened. The Baluch stood for a moment watching them silently and then in two swift strides, vanished inside Krishna Cottage.

Ignoring Gopal completely, Birju quickly unlocked his house and pushed open the door.

"Gopal babu! Why don't you come here?" he said, disappearing inside.

Gopal followed him in. The Baluch had made it very clear – no going out in the curfew and no carrying any baggage in the morning. What was the point then of unlocking his house? The Baluch soldiers occupied their lane and beyond that were the rioting mobs. Here, it was just Birju and himself. Might as well stick together. What was the point in being alone in the house?

He closed the door behind him. "Don't lock the door," the Baluch had said. What if he came to check? Wisdom lay in obeying. It would cost him nothing to shoot them.

He came and stood in the courtyard.

Birju saw him and also came out. He was probably hiding in the bathroom. His face was ashen and his eyes were still wide with fear.

"He won't kill us, will he?" he asked softly.

"Wipe your nose, it's running," said Gopal.

Gopal walked slowly to the drawing room.

This was Lalaji's *'baithak'*. He had ceremoniously hung pictures of his two wives on the walls.

"Gopal babu! He..."

He looked at Birju. He had followed him into the drawing room. Probably he still wanted to know if the soldier would kill them or not.

Gopal had seen Birju around for the last two years or so, ever since he had come to Lalaji's as a servant. But he had never observed him so closely before. Had he been dressed in clean clothes, this twelve or thirteen year old 'pahadi' boy would perhaps have been considered pretty. His colour was fair, his nose straight and sharp and, God knows from where he had got those pale blue eyes. But now he hung around him like a terrified rabbit.

"Look Birju," Gopal told him firmly, "you know we have to spend the night here. We can't starve ourselves, can we? Now you go and cook something and just forget about the soldier and his gun."

"Food? I'm very frightened of the Baluch, Gopal babu," he sniffed, wiping his eyes with the back of his hand, "let's get out of here first, and I'll cook you something as soon as we reach the camp."

"Birju, just listen to me," Gopal explained, "it won't help to be scared. We have to spend the night here somehow. If we manage till morning we might be able to make our way back. If we try to escape at night, then – bang! We are simply dead meat."

"Bang!" Birju uttered involuntarily. His eyes widened with terror and he slumped onto the floor. Even in the cold, beads of sweat broke out on his face. Uncomprehending, he just stared at Gopal.

Gopal was anxious enough as it was. The sight of the terrified boy simply made it worse. If it were known that these two were still in this house… anyone could sprinkle petrol or kerosene and set the house on fire. Even if the house weren't burnt, one thrust with a knife would be enough. Or may be a bullet from the Baluch's gun… he had said … "if you are alive till morning!" Will we survive till morning or not? And to top it all, Birju in this state…!

Last night, when a huge mob had attacked their locality, the elaborate arrangements of the committee for local security had collapsed in a moment. The committee volunteers had responded timidly with shouts of 'Jai Bajrang Bali!' when the mob had thundered, 'Allah-o-Akbar!' They could put up no resistance at all. As soon as the two houses were set ablaze, everyone fled.

At that time, no one had probably taken along a thing. Getting out alive was all that mattered, who could think of baggage! He could barely remember how he had made it to the camp with his sick mother. It had been a night of terror. But since morning, when things had stabilised somewhat, and the presence of the Dogra Regiment had instilled some confidence in the camp, a single thought tortured him. Mother had been sick for the last five years. Wouldn't it have been better if he had left her to die at home than to make her lie on the ground on a single sheet, given to them by the camp authority? At home, she would at least have been at peace till some rioter got her.

All day, he had watched his mother's discomfort, and all

day he had brooded. As evening fell, the prospect of the long night ahead and how to make mother comfortable haunted him. Sleeping on the sheet in these conditions, she would never make it through the night. There wasn't a soul in the camp who could give him a blanket or a sheet. On the spur of the moment, he decided to return home. He was sure somehow that their homes would neither have been burnt down nor looted. They would be securely locked the way they had left them yesterday.

He had wanted a couple of others to come with him but having barely escaped with their lives, no one was ready to return. Only Lalaji, his neighbour, had sent his servant Birju along, to pick up a few of his clothes. Either Birju had been unable to disobey his master or perhaps, he had no idea how risky it was to go back home… either way, happy to have company, Gopal hadn't said no…

Catching him by the hand, Gopal hauled Birju up, "get up… you! What's wrong with you, are you crazy?"

"Babuji! Gopal babu!" he babbled, and his legs buckled under him, refusing to hold him up.

Using all his strength, Gopal pulled him up. "Get up! Stand!"

He stood up. At that instant Gopal and Birju both looked at his wet pajama. Gopal now understood why he had resisted standing up.

"Go! Change your clothes," Gopal ordered angrily.

"I don't have any other clothes." Probably Birju was crying, "just yesterday Lalaji had promised that he would get some stitched for me."

Gopal felt really irritated. "Don't be mad! You've got the keys to everything. No one is going to stop you even if you wear Lalajli's woollen pant."

"What if Lalaji finds out?"

"Will Lalaji ever return, you fool!" exclaimed Gopal. "Everything will be abandoned in Pakistan. Put on whatever you can. Eat whatever you want. No one will say a thing. Everything is yours."

Gopal's words had a miraculous effect on the boy. The colour returned to his face and it seemed as if he was struggling to control his joy. A wicked gleam shone in his eyes. He had quite forgotten that fear had made him wet his pajamas just moments ago. He wanted desperately to say something but he would look up at Gopal, and each time, lower his eyes again.

"What is it?" Gopal asked.

"Shall I wear Lalaji's pants?"

Gopal looked at him briefly – so that's what it was. He didn't know whether to laugh or to feel angry at Birju's stupidity.

"Go on, wear it," he said.

"And what if Lalaji gets wild?"

"Tell him Gopal babu had told you to."

"And."

"Now what?" Gopal felt like giving him a good thrashing and asking him "you wretch, is this the time to fuss."

"And, and ..." he had the same strange smile on his face. "And shall I make pullao for myself also with fine basmati, the way I do for Lalaji?"

"Make it, you bastard, make it," Gopal told him through gritted teeth, his voice choked with anger. Birju glanced up and looked at him. Laughing softly he bounded off, rather like a boy whose mother has just given him money to buy himself an ice-cream in the lane.

Gopal turned once again to his own thoughts. If he couldn't make it back to the camp then what would be the fate of his sick mother? Wouldn't it be wiser to forget about her comfort and concentrate on his own survival. Mother had only a couple of years to live. His entire life lay ahead. In these disturbed, riot-torn times, planning the future was difficult, but surely there would ultimately be peace. They could make a new life for themselves in Hindustan. When Sarla learnt that he had left the camp to fetch mother's bedding and had not been seen since, what would she do? Sarla... in which camp might Sarla be?

And suddenly he smelt a strong aroma.... Was it *ghee*? Yes, the fragrance diffused all around was unmistakable, definitely pure *desi ghee*. Birju was probably cooking the pullao... the fool will get both of them killed. Anxiety gripped him. Why couldn't he make something simple that they could eat quickly and then lie low. Instead, he was spreading the fragrance of *ghee* everywhere, to advertise their presence and summon the rioters. What if a dagger should suddenly disembowel him and serve his intestines on a plate before him. Then he would enjoy his pullao!

Silently and swiftly he strode to Lalaji's kitchen. In this short span, Birju had been transformed. Without a care in the world, he squatted in the middle of the kitchen surrounded by spices, lentils, the vegetables bought yesterday, and several varieties of rice, as though he had been choosing from among them. Birju was frying onions on the stove with absolute concentration.

Suddenly aware of a presence in the kitchen he looked around, his eyes hesitant, skeptical. But in those eyes Gopal no longer saw the dread that he had seen in them a short while ago.

Birju looked through him as though unable to recognise him. Gradually recognition dawned. He laughed sheepishly. "I thought *Bibiji* has come. No wonder I couldn't make out why *Bibiji* was wearing *Lalaji's* pajamas instead of her own..."

Gopal had a mind to tell him, "you're scared of Bibiji and Lalaji, you rascal, not of the knife and gun!"

But he remained silent. Dressed in Lalaji's pant, free of all care, Birju sat in the middle of the kitchen. Had he been reminded of the Baluch standing outside he would most probably have soiled the kitchen too.

Gopal silently withdrew. Just as well, he needn't worry about Birju for now. He could think undisturbed and concentrate on the problem of getting back safely to the camp.

He was definite he did not want to wait here till morning. God only knew whether they'd be alive till then or not. But where was the sense in trying to make their way back in broad daylight. However, it would be good enough if in the darkness, they could give the Baluch the slip, and get across Trunkwala Bazaar. Because of the curfew, they would not meet a soul on the road outside. If they did encounter the police or the army and didn't try to run away, they would take them either to the jail up on the hill, or to the camp. In either case, they would be safe. But, if the Baluch saw them leaving through the narrow lane, he would know they were running away. Without a doubt, he would shoot them.

A tremor passed through him. Mother lying on the cold dirty floor with only a sheet under her flashed before him and then Sarla... Sarla in her wedding sari, the one with the pure gold border that she had made with her own hands.

"Gopal babu! Come! Come! Have your dinner!" He heard Birju's voice and jumped and stood up.

"Softly, you ass, softly!" he spluttered and raced into the kitchen.

Birju had laid out two huge plates. Heaps of the very finest long-grained fragrant rice! Swimming with *ghee* and spiced with cardamom, cinnamon, peas and coriander!

Gopal had never seen Birju so untroubled and blissful. He was in the seventh heaven. Birju chuckled on seeing him, "shall

I add some more *ghee*, Gopal babu?" he asked, dipping his hand into the tin of ghee.

"Enough! Enough!" he chided, "who will eat all this? You've sat down to a feast."

"Have some more, Gopal babu!" He had no idea of the fix they were in. "There's plenty more."

Gopal's mind was shrouded in gloom. He had no desire to eat. He almost refused the food but changed his mind. It was his idea to cook dinner and it would be odd if now he were to say he wasn't hungry.

"Just wait Gopal babu!" said Birju, hurriedly getting up, "I'd forgotten!"

Taken aback, he watched as Birju quickly scrambled up the stairs. He could hear his gentle humming from upstairs. Gopal's heart sank further… this boy's stupidity would surely land them in some mess today.

When Birju came down, in one hand was a jar of sweet and sour pickle and in the other, apple preserve.

"There's silver foil too. Shall I get some?" he asked. "We'll put it on the preserve."

"Sit right here!" He finally had to say, "don't you get too chirpy lest the Baluch get tempted to share your feast. He can fill your stomach with a single bullet!"

Birju wrinkled his nose distastefully. Two or three large mouthfuls of pullao, however, soon cheered him up. He had piled apple preserve and pickles on his plate. He continued eating steadily and swiftly.

"Birju!" Gopal said, "be careful you, don't make yourself sick."

"Don't you worry Babuji," he mumbled, his mouth full of rice. "Lalaji ate this everyday and never felt sick. In fact, watching him made me feel ill!"

"Just you listen!" Gopal said sharply, "we're not to sleep, we have to be up all night. We'll have to take turns keeping watch, and push off whenever we can. We must return to the camp tonight."

"Okay!" he responded, without the slightest interest, pouring two more spoonfuls of *ghee* onto his food.

"I can definitely hear some disturbance from the Bhabhdon ka mohalla. They will probably attack tonight. Some of them may show up here," Gopal warned him again.

"All right, all right!" he answered indifferently. Gulping down a glassful of water, he burped loudly and got down to eating again. The couple of mouthfuls that Gopal had eaten were already making him nauseous. He felt like retching. Had he eaten any more, he knew he would vomit. He stopped. He wouldn't eat any more. Getting up, he took water from the bucket and began washing his hands.

Gopal walked out into the courtyard. Gently opening the unlocked front door, he peered out. The lane was dark and deserted. The door of Krishna Cottage from which the Baluch had appeared was open. He could see a faint glow. Perhaps he had lighted a fire.

We can't leave that way – he thought.

At the other end of the lane were a couple of Gujjar houses. Faint sounds could be heard from there too. Going that way would be difficult. They had only one option. He had to go to Reshma Chachi's house. So what if she was a Muslim. How dearly she loved him. Besides, ever since her son Salaamat's death, she had as good as accepted Gopal as her own son… there was no other choice. Reshma Chachi's house was right next to those of the Gujjars. Now or may be later, at the right moment, she could if she wanted, send them off quietly…..

He shut the door gently and returned silently inside. Birju wasn't in the kitchen. He wasn't in the drawing room either. Gopal found him covered in a quilt in Lalaji's bedroom, lying on the luxuriously furnished bed. Lalaji's *hukka* was on the side table, and pipe in hand, Birju was smoking away contentedly. The enticing aroma of fine tobacco was perfuming the air.

"Birju!" Gopal just managed to suppress the scream of frustration emanating from his throat.

"Come, Gopal babu, come sit!" Birju moved over making space for him. "Have a smoke," he said offering him the pipe.

To Gopal it appeared that it was not *ghee* that Birju had consumed but opium. His eyes were drugged and he appeared half asleep. It was as though he had, with an immense effort, emerged from a deep sleep or drugged *state* and his eyelids were ready to drop once again.

Gopal glared at him. But it had no effect. Birju had already sunk back into slumber. The faint bubbling of the *hukka* indicated that, just as a baby suckles while asleep, he continued to draw involuntarily on the *hukka* pipe in his sleep.

"Birju, we aren't to sleep," he bent down and said in his ear. "We are to keep watch all night."

"Okay," answered Birju, still in his drugged state. "We'll do that. Just let me rest a while first," and turning over, he was fast asleep again.

THE TRANSFORMATION

Anuradha arrived terribly late. When she finally did, she was acutely depressed.

Amitabh wanted to ask her right away – why so late, and why so sad? But he knew Anuradha only too well. Most conveniently she would shift all the blame onto the transport system. And the depression? Anuradha would not tell. Every time he had asked, it had been the same answer, "nothing's happened. Why do you hassle me over nothing at all?"

Amitabh was silent.

From Maurice Nagar, they were headed towards the University Library, in complete silence.

Anuradha suddenly spoke up, "listen Amit! I want to tell you something; but promise, you won't ask any questions."

Anuradha was spilling the beans herself. Where was the need for him to dig for information? He knew she wouldn't be able to hide anything from him. She would tell him a little at first, and by the time she left, everything would be told.

Just to please her, he said, "I won't ask."

He had thought that she would immediately launch into her narrative, and stop only when she had told him everything.

But she was silent again. Her silence was a real strain on his nerves.

As they climbed up the library stairs, Amitabh stood at one side. Anuradha went to the counter. It took her only five minutes to return the books. Dropping the cards into her bag and adjusting the *pallu* of her sari, she walked into the library stack-hall. Amitabh had to go along. He didn't like this at all. What had she been about to tell him? How long was he supposed to wait? He wanted to get out of here as quickly as possible so that he could ask her. But she was in no hurry. She would select four or five books, get them issued, and only then would she leave the library. All this would take at least half an hour.

Anuradha was scanning the shelves. Meanwhile, Amitabh hung around, gazing casually at the others in the stack. Anuradha chose three books and fishing out the cards from her bag, gestured for him to follow. Walking ahead, Amitabh headed straight out of the door and stood on the steps outside. She was soon by his side.

"Now what's the matter?" Amitabh asked as soon as they had gone down the stairs.

"I'll tell you," Anuradha said. She really wasn't trying to put him off.

He guessed he would have to ask her a couple of times more.

Walking past the Law Faculty, they came and stood outside Ramjas College. By then he had already asked her a couple of times again. She wanted to tell him, but skirting around the issue in her usual way, she chatted on about all kinds of other things. When she reached the main road just near the Delhi School, she suddenly stood still.

"Oh no! I've forgotten it again."

"What have you forgotten?" Amitabh felt irritated.

"Just look! We have come all the way here," she said, "we could as well have met Mrs. Sharma."

"Why not meet her then! Who told you not to?"

"Not today. I haven't brought her things today."

"Forget it then. Now, what was it you were going to tell me?"

"What thing." Anuradha paused for a moment, "don't misunderstand and don't ask any questions."

"I won't!"

"Look," she said very softly, "you'd better stop coming over to our place. We can meet anywhere else, whenever you say, I'll come. But we won't meet at home."

"Why?" Amitabh blurted out.

"You said you wouldn't ask," she reminded him.

"Okay! Okay! I won't ask."

They walked along silently for a while.

"Are you upset?"

"No, what's there to be upset about," Amitabh said.

Anuradha looked at his face – he didn't appear to be worried.

A huge load was off Amitabh's mind. From the moment Anuradha had told him so earnestly that she had something to tell, the words of her *mausi* were echoing through his mind.

Amitabh had met Anuradha's aunt only once but he had heard a great deal about her from Anuradha. Mausi was awfully rich. They owned a couple of coal mines. Both her sons were in the US and her daughter was married to some minister's son. She had come out with a whole string of matches for Anuradha, each more desirable than the next. Most exceptional matches: highly educated handsome sons of wealthy parents, and all of them holding the best of jobs!

Amitabh had taken an instant dislike to this aunt. And he feared her too. Soon after he had begun to have those dreadful nightmares of a witch carrying Anuradha away from him. He would shout and struggle but he was fixed to the spot and couldn't stir an inch. And the witch: unfailingly, she had Mausi's face.

Anuradha had taken a sweetly malicious pleasure in laughing at Amitabh's fears. Her logic was simple. Mausi only recommended families suited to *her* standards, she never considered the status of Anuradha's parents. So her plans would never work out, would they? Besides, couldn't he give her credit for being an independent adult? She wasn't a child who would promptly marry any old boy that her aunt would suggest!

They had walked along quietly for quite a while now. Amitabh looked up at her but her face gave away nothing. He knew she wasn't going to say anything further in a hurry. But the cloud that had shadowed her face since morning had lifted simply by talking about it.

"Well, where are we going anyway?" he asked smiling, trying to show her how relaxed he felt.

Anuradha stopped and looked at him, "suppose we go to Connaught Place? We can shop a bit and have coffee somewhere!"

He walked on silently. They took an auto from Malkaganj.

Strolling along the Connaught Place verandah, Amitabh was wondering, if he wasn't supposed to visit Anuradha's home, where was he to meet her now? He didn't really fancy the scenario of seeing her regularly at any old place. But, if he didn't do that, where would they meet? He couldn't dream of not meeting her every day but he was distressingly sure that someone wanted to put his mettle to test.

Amitabh stopped at Handloom House. Turning around, Anuradha looked at him, a question mark over her face.

"Anu!" He felt his voice tremble.

Anuradha moved close to him.

"Our love faces its first hurdle today! It wants to measure the depth of our love. I must give you something today!"

Taking Anuradha by the arm, he led her inside the showroom. He knew he was being rather theatrical, but he didn't try to check himself.

Anuradha picked up a simple white cotton sari with a broad red border. He paid for it, and then they sat for a delightfully long time at the Shamiana Coffee House.

When Amitabh got home, he was depressed. This was clearly the thin edge of the wedge. Today the restriction of meeting her at home, tomorrow it could be anything else. He could no longer survive without seeing her. How could he let this happen? Was he really so spineless? He needed to do some genuine soul-searching.

When the question of marriage had first been broached, Anuradha and he were complete strangers. At that stage, a hoard of relations had been involved. He could now no longer remember how and when the routine chit-chat had changed into romance. He found it difficult now to imagine a time when he had come formally to 'see' her or that he had been invited to do so. It had been so natural for them to choose each other without the slightest conscious effort.

They had been going out, whenever they felt like it. They saw films together. He would buy the tickets, call up from the cinema hall, and even if one of the elders picked up the phone, he would tell them that he was speaking from the hall, that he had bought the tickets and would they please send Anuradha. And every time, Anuradha came. No one ever objected. Several times they had dinner together and many times he would head straight for Anuradha's place from his office. He would then naturally have his evening tea there. He would tell them neither of his coming nor did he need an invitation. They all simply knew that he would come. Actually, the day he didn't show up, they were sure to ask why he hadn't made it. When he was so completely committed to Anuradha, why this restriction now?

When it was time to leave, Amitabh realised they had not decided where to meet next and when. But he didn't ask. Anuradha had told him not to come, so why not let her decide what they would do. He knew she looked forward to their meetings. It wasn't a one-sided thing at all. Anuradha waited desperately for him, so why couldn't she take the initiative?

But Anuradha didn't touch on this at all. She was busy admiring the new sari. Every now and then she clutched the packet to her chest and even raised it to her lips. Lost in her thoughts, Anuradha had left and nothing had been decided. His head was aching and he could feel his heart sink.

By morning, gloom had enveloped his soul. It was as though a syringe had been stuck into him and every drop of energy drained. Just getting up from bed seemed an impossible effort. But he had to go to office. Busy at work, he would forget Anuradha and feel better. Lying around like this would only make things worse.

He ate his breakfast. By the time, he dressed he had changed his mind. First to the University and then to the office, he decided. He would be late, but he had to go to the University first, fix up their evening rendezvous and then race to work. Anuradha was invariably in the library by ten and he had to be in his seat by nine thirty. He would be late all right, but what the hell, he had to meet her.

Sharp at ten he met her in the library.

"You've come? You haven't gone to the office? I was wondering where to call you. If we hadn't met now I'd have come to your room in the evening."

"Office!" Amitabh laughed, "I'll just go."

"It's already ten?"

"Yes!"

"This order's made it tough, hasn't it?"

"Yes Anu!" he answered quickly, "where'll we meet in the evening?"

"In the evening?" Anuradha thought for a moment, "come to Wengers then we'll work it out."

"Okay," Amitabh said, "I'll be off, it's getting late".

And without waiting for an answer, he walked out of the library. Now he could face his work, he felt better already.

After the office, he didn't wait for a bus, it might be half an hour before one showed up. Just ten minutes of brisk walking from Parliament Street and he would be at Wengers.

Anuradha was sitting by herself at the corner table. She had just arrived and hadn't ordered yet.

He put the magazines down on the table and sprawled comfortably on his chair. Anuradha looked up at him and smiled gently.

"Coming from the University?"

"No!" Anuradha said, "think I'd wear this sari and go to the University?"

She was wearing the new white, red-border sari.

"Been home?"

"Yes, I've been home," she said, "I've changed my sari and I've fought and come."

"Fought?"

"Yes", Anuradha explained, "everyone was pretty impressed when I wore it. Wanted to know from where I had got it. I'm not scared of anyone, I told them. Mummy was wild at me. 'We aren't paupers you know, that you need to take saris from Amitabh,' she said, 'once you're married, you take whatever you like from him, but you are not to take anything from him now.' She asked me to return it, but how could I? I told her I wouldn't and that I was going to wear it and then go out to meet you."

"So the first time we meet outside the home and the squabbles have begun?" Amitabh smiled.

"Naturally! That's bound to happen. After all, they started it all. Let's forget it," and changing the topic, "what're you getting us to eat?"

They had their sandwiches and coffee and paying the bill, they walked out.

"How about a movie?" Amitabh asked.

"It'll get late Ami! I didn't tell them I'd be late."

"But that isn't necessary."

"All right, let's go."

For an hour or so she was okay, but after that Amitabh could sense she wasn't enjoying the film. She was distracted and restless. Several times he softly asked her what the matter was, but she avoided telling him.

"How was it?" Amitabh asked, as they came out of the hall.

"To tell you the truth," she answered unenthusiastically, "I didn't enjoy it. I hadn't told them at home and I don't like staying out late without telling them. My heart wasn't in it."

Amitabh could understand her feelings. "Come, I'll drop you home in a cab." Anuradha didn't fuss.

"Can I ask you something, Ami?" She said as the taxi started.

"Sure!" he didn't like her to be off mood like this.

"How much have you spent today?"

"Five at Wengers, seven fifty for the film and..."

"Another five for the taxi!" Anuradha calculated, "don't you think it's awfully expensive meeting like this?"

"So what?" he said unfazed, "what's the harm if one spends once in a while."

"Ya, that's okay but we'll have to meet like this every day and to spend so much daily..."

"Tell you what," Amitabh said, "tomorrow's an off. Meet me at the Odeon stop after lunch. We'll go to Qutub. Heaps of space to roam around, it'll be fun and no expense either!"

"Okay," Anuradha said and then fell silent.

Amitabh saw the strained look on her face, she didn't relax for a moment, just sat there all tensed up.

"What's wrong, Anu? Don't you like the plan?"

"No, it's not that," she burst out, "I don't like meeting like this. We were perfectly happy sitting around at home. But now..." she paused, "I'm mad at my folks for chucking us out of the house like this."

Amitabh was silent. He felt it too. Always meeting outside just didn't seem natural. Seeing her at home filled him with a deep sense of happiness and now there wasn't a trace of it. Even Anuradha seemed different. Earlier he would drop by, they would sit chatting till late. When he tried to leave, how earnestly Anuradha would beg him to stay on. Now she just wants to run off home, not a minute extra. Even while she was with him, he felt no sense of joy because this togetherness itself was a sort of compulsion.

He feared that Anuradha wasn't the only one who felt angry with her family. Even he was resentful. If the two of them allowed this anger to build up they would needlessly feel alienated. What if things didn't get sorted even after they were married, he may always feel that he hadn't married Anuradha but had eloped with her. And that when Anuradha's father had himself chosen him. The choosing, their meeting regularly, everything was with his approval then why the tension now? He wasn't happy about this at all.

Stopping the taxi, Amitabh dropped Anuradha off, outside her house reminding her of their plan for Qutub. Normally he would have sent off the cab and walked her home, met everyone and probably had dinner there as well. Today he didn't get off. Waving from the cab, he left.

Anuradha too made no effort to linger or urge him to stop. Waving her hand she turned and went in.

The following day Anuradha was totally off mood.

"Fought again?" Amitabh joked.

"Yes!" she said, "but don't ask. I'll tell you at Qutub."

The bus was so packed they couldn't sit together nor could they chat. For the next hour and a half, they sat separately, together only in the knowledge that they were in the same bus.

They got off at Qutub. The grounds were flooded with hoards of holiday-makers, not a bit of privacy at all. They didn't pause anywhere…just kept moving.

"What happened, Anu?" Amitabh asked.

"They … nothing particular really. You know Vinita's taken a fancy to the red-bordered sari. Wanted to wear it out somewhere, I refused her. I've never stopped her from using anything, but this is different. It's your gift, a symbol of our love. How could I let anyone else wear it, even if it is my own sister?"

"Then?"

"Then what, mayhem! Vinita was all cut up, so I ticked her off and she began crying. That upset Mummy and she told me to give her the sari. I refused. You know what she said? 'Such a precious sari as if she's going to wear it for her *pheras*. Couldn't be worth more than twenty rupees.' That did it. I told her, 'all right, then I'll get married only in this sari.' That was right, wasn't it! No objections?"

Amitabh was stunned. He didn't think she would go that far and want his approval too. "But Anu, this sari is white," he said, "don't you wear red for the wedding?"

"I don't care about that," Anuradha retorted. "This sari is what I'll wear. Red's considered auspicious so everyone wears red. This has a red border anyway and if I think it's lucky, what's the problem? You tell me right now if you have any hang-ups."

Amitabh didn't have the courage to object. What if she turned on him? If she wanted to give the said so much importance, what could he say? After all she was acknowledging his love for her.

"So madam's in a great hurry for the *pheras*, is it?" Amitabh said, changing the topic.

It didn't have the desired effect. Anuradha was as solemn as ever, even more determined than before. "Yes Ami, I'm really fed up now! My own dearest, seeing you briefly like this feels awful. We should be together all the time, twenty-four hours a day. But that can only happen after we're married."

Amitabh also sobered up. "I've been wondering Anu ever since yesterday, there's no point in delaying the wedding. Getting out everyday, dodging people and meeting briefly like this is no fun at all."

They didn't hang around Qutub for long. They didn't feel at ease there among all those family groups. The two of them, quite clearly not married, it didn't seem right to either of them.

To find a secluded spot, they had to go into the jungle a bit and that was risky.

After this there was a long break in their lives. They hardly met at all and when they did they were rarely alone. There would be something to discuss or a decision to take and they would do just that and then separate. His single room would no longer be enough. He had to hunt for a house, put a whole household together, get the wedding cards printed, shop for a hundred other things, book the buses for the *baraat*. There were so many things to do…the list was endless. And then go around and distribute the wedding cards, prepare for the reception. It was another matter of course that Anuradha was often with him, but that peculiar dazed state in which the work had been done, how could he count that as a part of his life! Amitabh no longer felt like Amitabh, and Anuradha like Anuradha! Two cogs in the machine who mechanically did what had to be done and that was all…

Those days! What a tussle there had been in the world within him and around him. Filed at so many places, he had become utterly smooth, perfect like a pebble. Facing numberless situations, a brand new world of people, wherever he was touched one more edge, another jagged spur would be worn away till he had been rendered round, even and boring. It seemed as though all had crumbled. His own identity, like the dust and chips had been lost along the way. The sharp edges of his personality, which he had nurtured so painstakingly over the years, had worn away. This crumbling, this wearing away had been accomplished, sometimes to satisfy the wishes of his family, at others to accommodate Anuradha's folks. Amitabh had been unable to resist for he had wanted to displease no one.

On an auspicious pundit-approved day, astride a white horse, and resplendent in wedding regalia, accompanied by lights and a band, he had arrived in a procession at Anuradha's doorstep. *Milni* had been followed by *sehra* and *jaymala* and then the feast.

Seated for the *pheras*, Amitabh had sensed the special bond between the two sisters that day. Vinita was constantly by Anuradha's side adjusting a pleat here, straightening her *chunni* there. The wedding rituals were soon done with, and Anuradha was whisked indoors to emerge in the pink sari she would wear to her new home.

Next to him in the car was again some new Anuradha, a stranger who felt no attachment for him. He sat there right next to her and not once had she glanced up at him. He soothed her gently as she silently wept. This must be some other Anuradha, it could not be the one who had never hesitated to boldly acknowledge her love for him.

Once alone the old Anuradha returned. She wiped away her tears and smiled.

"You cried all the way," Amitabh said, "upset coming here Anu?"

"Couldn't help it, the tears just came," she hesitatingly said, "but I'm not sad about coming here. Right from morning today, things were a mess at home. You have no idea Ami what happened!"

"What?"

"Ami, you know I wore your red-bordered white sari for the *pheras*," she said in a deeply emotional tone. "They did of course wrap another sari over it. Vinita made sure this stayed in place every moment. I've come here wrapped in your love... you will promise me one thing Ami?"

"What?" Amitabh was amazed. Tonight he could refuse her nothing.

"Ami, wrap me in this sari when I die!"

"Anu!" Shocked, Amitabh held her close, "don't ever speak of such a thing Anu! I understand what you feel."

Anuradha cried for quite some time while Amitabh comforted here. Amitabh could not remember when they had finally slept.

Travelling about for that month in the hills, time simply flew past. Back in Delhi, he sensed a new serenity within himself. A sign perhaps of a new born contentment that had replaced the old restlessness.

A new home, a fresh environment brought for Anuradha a fresh status and its own responsibilities. These seemed to envelop her completely. Often enough it hurt her to realise, that as Anuradha she was nothing. Now her only identity was as Amitabh's wife. She didn't like it at all, this insensitivity to her individuality, but whenever she tried to assert her independent will, it invariably clashed with Amitabh's.

She had desired a husband in the role of a helper. One who would select her clothes and lay them out on the bed when she went for her bath, run and get her sari ironed if she had to go out, and put out the appropriate jewellery from the cupboard. When she left for work, he should tidy the room, hang up her nightclothes, make the bed and spread her towel on the line outside. Replace the cap on the bottle of oil, put the puff back in the powder box and clean the comb and push it back into the brush. The glass and empty teacup should be returned to the kitchen. And when she returned home in the evening, he should pay off the auto downstairs and place before her a glass of water, a cup of tea or perhaps some sliced fruit. At bed-time he should fold the bedcover, dust the bed and when she had fallen asleep, draw the blanket over her.

But Amitabh was nothing like that at all. Whatever he may have been before, now he was her husband and he had no intention of being his wife's assistant. She discovered soon enough that his expectations of her were identical to her's.

Soon after, Anuradha had begun feeling unwell. She lost her appetite and whatever she managed to eat, she threw up. Her blood pressure was up and her feet were swollen. And she had no stamina at all. She grew irritable. She would quarrel over the slightest thing and then cry for hours.

Then his father had written to say it would be better if he sent Anuradha home. There she would be well looked after. They had no experience in such matters and were alone in Delhi and no one wanted anything to go wrong.

At first he hesitated. How could he live without Anuradha? When she had asked him not to visit her at home he had almost had a nervous breakdown at the thought of not seeing her daily. Now he would have to send her away for months on end. But here together they weren't particularly happy either. Every day they would quarrel over some thing or the other. He consulted Anuradha and sensed that she would rather go.

Anuradha left for Kanpur.

For the first few days, life seemed pointless. As though he had nothing to do. Once married, everything revolved around home and he had no moorings outside and no place where he could spend his time. He had fallen into a peculiar routine. Off to office in the morning. A wife at home to attend to all his needs. Home cooked food, dusting and cleaning the house on Sundays. He had become so domesticated that long absence from home became an impossibility.

Then came a spell when he began to feel stressed. He was getting to be touchy. Once again his heart-beat would echo in his ears and there was this burning sensation in his chest. Was he heading for a nervous breakdown again?

Anuradha's letters came every week. She had been to the doctor's, her blood test had been done and she was swallowing a handful of capsules every day. She was drinking her milk every day, an egg too and plenty of fruit. These weren't Anuradha's letters to Amitabh, merely a wife's bulletins to her husband.

But then, he didn't miss Anuradha much either. It was the lack of a wife, without whom countless needs went unfulfilled, that troubled him. If someone else, not Anuradha, had been his wife, would it actually have made a difference? He would have loved her just as much, because a husband is supposed to love his wife. These weren't his feelings, only his obligations to domesticity. He was incredibly weak-minded, his lack of character masquerading as idealism. He could not go elsewhere to satisfy his physical needs and so he constantly yearned for his wife. He needed a wife and so he loved her, and wasn't it natural to love one who satisfied one's needs?

Did he then not love Anuradha? Or did Anuradha not love him? Was it only an arrangement to fulfill physical and social needs? Would it then have made all that much of a difference if they had not met and chosen each other? If his needs found satisfaction somewhere else would he no longer require Anuradha? Or were Anuradha to find her needs otherwise fulfilled would she cease to love him? What would then become of that red-bordered sari...

Amitabh didn't want to arrive at any conclusion. All he wanted was for the days to pass somehow till Anuradha's return, and the load be off his mind and there would be no need to think of such things.

There was plenty of time for Anuradha's return and he knew he would have to manage any how on his own.

As long as he was at home his attention was rivetted to the front door. He would hear a sound at the door, and there would be no one there. He knew it was his desires that deluded his ears. He wanted someone, anyone to come, but why? May be it would help the time pass easily or was it because he was alone at home. Not even the servant was around. He was utterly alone. Who was he waiting for then? If it was a specific person he could have gone and visited, then who could he be waiting for in this desolate house...?

When the bell rang that day he was taken aback to see an unknown woman outside. Looking questioningly at her he asked, "what is it?"

"Do you need vim?" she stammered.

"Certainly not!"

"You don't use vim?" she asked with considerable effort.

He slammed the door shut.

She was new to this profession, very hesitant, how red in the face she was. But why was he so restless? Why had he banged the door? Who had he been afraid of? He could easily have lured her into the house. These independent flats, no one would have a clue, and he was quite alone... he flushed hot... she wasn't at all pretty but then she was young. She had shown up at his door and he was alone at home. He had willfully shut the door and turned her away... then why was he regretting it?

That's not done, he thought. Anuradha is his wife, he loved her. He should not harbour such thoughts about anyone else. He ought to be ashamed of himself. What would Anuradha say if she knew? But he knew it was not fear of her but fear of himself that made him do it... and if he truly loved Anuradha, then why did the sight of an unknown woman at his door make his pulse race...?

It was after a long and eager wait that he got the news. "Congratulations! It's a baby boy." So many questions about the baby crowding into his mind but uppermost was one simple thought – he could now bring Anuradha home. It had been such a long time; to stay further would be pointless. He quickly calculated – twenty-one days and all the rituals would be over, on the twenty-second day they could set off. He wrote to his father saying he would fetch Anuradha on the twenty-second day and would he do their bookings please. And as for him, he would reach Kanpur at the appropriate time.

He spent the interim time scoring out the days on the calendar. In Kanpur, he was reunited with Anuradha and the baby. There was nothing extraordinary. Like all mothers Anuradha held the child to her breast and fed him. The baby clung to her and suckled, an ordinary baby that managed to look quite fetching when it smiled, but more often, when crying, looked ugly and repulsive.

In this spell of time Anuradha had become quite shrewd. She would carefully put away the baby's new sheets and blankets, nappies and frocks. The baby lay around in used, worn out clothes. Still so tiny, it soiled everything. She would use only the old clothes that would be left behind in Kanpur, why spoil the new stuff. She would rather save them for Delhi.

Everything was ready. He did get a day in Kanpur but that went in planning for the journey. They would have to spend the night in the train and the baby wasn't well either. He had got severe diarrohoea. They had packed the medicines but they would take their time, they weren't magical after all. Mother gave Anuradha plenty of instructions. Father advised Amitabh and then they were off.

Everything was fine. They had a coupe to themselves, but as the train moved the wind turned chilly. Anuradha wrapped the baby carefully and Amitabh got up and shut all the windows.

The train was on its way. The two of them now alone, all on their own and the shutters down. Suddenly, Amitabh's body was on fire. He cradled Anuradha's face in his hands but Anuradha sat cold and statue-like. There was no response from her.

Controlling his surging desires, he asked, "why are you so glum, Anu?"

"He's not well," she looked at the baby.

"He'll be fine in Delhi," Amitabh assured her, "we'll take him to a good doctor."

He sat up close to Anuradha, but he could sense the heat pulsating only through his body.

The baby had soiled his nappy; Anuradha wiped him with it and put him into a fresh one. Dangling the dirty diaper between her finger and thumb she looked around vaguely.

"What is it?" Amitabh wanted her to finish with all this quickly so that he could sit with her and show her how much he had missed her.

"What shall I do with this?" she asked indicating the dirty nappy with her eyes.

"Go wash it."

"You're joking!" Anuradha replied pertly, "he'll keep messing all night and I'll keep washing them?"

"Throw it away then." There was an edge of sharpness to his voice.

Anuradha looked up and stared at him. Her eyes were utterly expressionless. "If I start throwing them away, there won't be a single napkin left by the time we reach Delhi."

Amitabh stared back at her, "then what will you do?"

Anuradha thought for a bit and said, "I'll chuck this one in any case."

Lifting the shutter slightly she flung the diaper out. Turning around, she said, "just pull out this trunk and open it."

"What do you need this for now?" He couldn't hide his irritation.

"I'll pull out some old garment," Anuradha replied, "I'll tear it up into squares. I can throw these rags away when they're dirty."

Unwillingly he got to his feet and dragging the trunk out, opened the lock. Lifting up the lid, he said, "here, fish it out".

Anuradha rummaged through the clothes. Right on top were her heavy wedding silks. Pulling them out she heaped them on the berth. And then, from the bottom of the trunk, she pulled out a red-bordered white sari... holding it up she looked at it closely and said, "this will be fine."

Amitabh stared at the sari and felt sickened from within. Without a word he picked up sari after sari and threw it back into the box. Stuffing everything in, he locked the trunk and kicking it with his feet pushed it under the berth.

He turned to look at Anuradha. She was busy elsewhere. She had torn out a neat square from the sari. She folded it into a perfect triangle and, utterly engrossed, she put it on for the baby.

Swallowing the spittle in his mouth, he silently climbed onto the upper berth. He did not have the guts to look down at the scene below. All night he listened to the ripping of the sari and the clatter of the shutter, raised each time Anuradha threw out a soiled napkin. Not a word was spoken.

It was Anuradha who called out in the morning, "get up I say! We're almost there."

He climbed down. Not looking at Anuradha he began to gather up their things. He closed the suitcase, rolled up the bedding and dusting his hands, stood up.

"Just check," Anuradha said, "in case we've left anything behind."

He checked the upper berth first, where he had spent the night. Then he bent and looked under the lower berth. He saw some cloth-like thing dangling below. Stretching under the berth he pulled it out. It was a red border. Throughout the night, the white sari had perhaps been torn, bit by bit, into square pieces, and thrown out of the window.

His jaw set grimly, Amitabh raised the shutter with his left hand and with his right hand, flung the red border far out somewhere.

Slowly inching its way into the station, the train came to a halt at platform number eleven of Delhi Junction.

BEFORE WE GO TO SLEEP

He must have looked at his watch for the hundredth time. Restlessly, he paced up and down. He had glanced at the clock on the table again and again, but nothing eased his mind. Every few minutes, he went to the front door and then came back in. He resolved to set out again and again, but each time he abandoned the idea and came back to sit on the sofa or stretch out on the divan. Nothing was helping.

In the end, he finally went and changed his clothes. He got into his trousers and shirt and put on his shoes. As he sat wiping these with a duster, he decided – he must set out, it was not possible for him to wait any longer.

Suddenly, he thought of his wallet: only a couple of rupees in it - that wouldn't do. He might need to go far; may be, all the way to Sheela's office. At this hour, he would probably have to take a taxi. A bus wasn't really quite the right transport when one was going out to search for someone!

He took out five teners from the locker. It was quite possible that he might need to spend on something else besides the taxi. Involuntarily, the image of the emergency room of a large hospital began to flash through his mind; he saw himself pacing through night-darkened markets in search of 24-hour chemist shops.

He gave himself a shake. Why on earth was he giving in to foolish thoughts! Picking up the lock, he walked briskly to the front door. He bolted the door, but before he locked up, he paused for a moment.

Had he decided where he would go at this time of the night? Would he go around staring at each female form that he encountered and, in the dark, fail to recognise even a single one. Was something wrong with his eyes, he wondered, maybe he should get his spectacles checked... actually, it could be that everyone faced this problem ... he couldn't recognise anyone from a distance but, as they came close, they would always look like the person he was looking for.

Worried sick like he was tonight, last time he had set out to hunt for Sheela, she had arrived home just as he had set off. By the time he returned, he had spent a good 15 rupees on a taxi and roamed about pointlessly all over the place. As for Sheela, she had been bored to tears, waiting for him in the verandah.

Then, they had had a fight, a *battle royale* it had been. Why was it that Sheela made it so late coming home from the office when she knew he got all bothered and tense. That was what infuriated him. And Sheela, she was fed up with his nervousness. She wasn't going out to roam around, was she? She was doing a job, and one could get late, couldn't one? You come home tired and worn out, and find the place locked up? Then?

It would be better if he waited a little longer. Sheela just might get home soon enough. It was a huge city and such a worthless transport system! Getting late wasn't such a rare thing, either. Why should he always imagine that some disaster was always lurking around to pounce on Sheela so that he could rush to her rescue and save her ... no, he really must wait a little longer.

As he waited, he saw a shadowy figure turn towards their quadrangle, walking a little slowly – in a tired, exhausted sort of way. It might even be Sheela. It was definitely a woman. As she came closer he was convinced it was Sheela – and, it actually was.

A huge load fell off his mind. It was very late but at least Sheela was back. As for getting late – it could always happen at work. He felt he was relieved for another reason too. He didn't have to wander out in the darkened streets, peering at strange anxiety-ridden faces, seeing beyond the mask to gaze into unknown eyes. He had been saved a great deal of trouble.

He felt mildly irritated. Why doesn't Sheela realise that he worried about her…

Sheela glanced at him with eyes that wore an odd expression, and without saying a word or pausing near him, she crossed the verandah and went indoors. She stopped, neither to tell him of her troubles, nor to explain what had happened. She didn't even come meekly to stand near him as a penitent, ready to accept her guilt and listen to his scolding…

His gaze followed Sheela indoors and hovered there uncertainly, just as hers had done. She did not speak. She didn't seem to be in a mood to listen. She hadn't even gone and dumped herself on the sofa as though nothing had happened. Something had definitely happened but she had perhaps not made up her mind how exactly she was going to tell him about it.

Exasperation gave his voice a knife-like edge, "you…"

"Yes! I'm back." Her voice emerged from some hidden depth, some unknown place from which she had never spoken before. Then, as if to taunt him, she asked, "I've got late, haven't I?"

Like a lizard, his annoyance slithered away. "Yes, it is very late. But you've…"

"You didn't go to look for me?" Sheela's tone was acutely sarcastic.

He flushed. Perhaps Sheela was mocking at his sentimentality. He pulled himself together. What was wrong in any case if he did get worried like this about his wife! How could Sheela tease him about this? He told her simply, "I was just thinking of setting out. See, I've just picked up the lock and key."

"It kept getting later and later, and you were only thinking?" Sheela's tone had grown even more somber.

He glared at Sheela angrily. She too was staring straight at him. He could clearly see the scratches on her face and forehead, the bruises and black marks of injury…he turned cold with fear… her hair was disheveled and, just like her hair, her clothes…could it be that Sheela had landed up among the wrong sort of men? No, perhaps not… he kept warning her everyday about moving buses and pushing crowds…

"What's happened to you?" That was all he could manage.

It was as though Sheela had suddenly let go. So far, she had probably been working out how she would face him. Now, she was facing him.

"You worried every day, didn't you, that an accident might happen and I used to assure you. Well…"

"Then, it's happened today, hasn't it? You don't know how worried I've been." He came towards her, "You haven't been hurt too badly, have you. Let me apply something, dettol…"

His voice became tender, the words seeking to soothe her wounds.

She didn't utter a word. She moved forward and sat on the sofa, "no, nothing that needs dettol…I'm so tired."

She shut her eyes and stretched herself on the sofa.

He sensed that they had covered the initial ground, come to a place where he could ask her about the incident and now Sheela would tell him. He came close, "but what actually happened?"

Sheela lay with her eyes closed and answered softly, "the usual bus business."

His suppressed irritation surfaced, "you tried to get on to a running bus didn't you…I've told you a hundred times…"

Sheela cut in, "No, I didn't tried to get on or get off a moving bus – I've understood what you've told me. Your advice doesn't go waste."

Her tone was so cold, so precise, that he felt stunned.

Steadying himself, he said, "then what happened? Did you lose your balance, fall down in the rush?"

For the first time, exasperation crept into her voice, "no, nothing like that."

"Then why on earth don't you tell me! You go and get yourself injured, and then you come home and lie down quietly like this. Why don't you say something, tell me something? Here I keep waiting for you, dying of worry and now, when I ask, I don't get an answer." There was a razor-edge to his voice.

Sheela's eyes flew open and she sat up as if she would definitely say something truly bitter. But her mood changed, she subsided, sinking into the sofa as abruptly as she had sat up. "I'll tell you, but get me a glass of water, please!"

He went inside to fetch the water and Sheela, rousing herself, sat up straight. Taking out the powder compact from her handbag, she carefully surveyed her face as though she were reviewing some bygone incident. Her fingers travelled gingerly over the scratches and bruises. It seemed as if she was truly registering them only now.

He had brought the water. Sheela snapped the compact shut, put it in her bag, and then closed the zip. She drank the water, carefully placed the glass on the peg table next to her, and lay down. Once again, her eyes were closed.

He waited, hoping that Sheela would speak to him. But, with eyes closed, she lay there utterly at peace though it was clear that there was a great deal going on inside her, chewing the cud, perhaps, of events... like the incessant rolling of some ancient film before her mind's eye. He couldn't bear it any longer, "you were about to tell me something."

Her upper lip twitched as though taunting him, "aren't you going to scold me for coming home so late? In our family, women don't hang around away from home like this, do they."

He was almost in tears. Sheela was making a mockery of his love. But he didn't shed any tears. What he really wanted to do at this moment, was to give her a long lecture with just a fine touch of drama, "surely you know that one's concern is in proportion to one's attachment. Whenever you get late, horrendous images begin to crowd my mind. I see you trying to catch a bus, running there right in the middle of the road, and some other bus or car comes, knocking you down. You lie there, wallowing in blood and no one comes near you. Or, you're standing at the bus stop and waiting and waiting and waiting … but not a single bus arrives. It's ten thirty, then eleven, and then eleven thirty … and then, you're overcome by some disaster."

But he didn't say any of these things. "When you get late I imagine the most frightening things," was all that he said.

"You imagine these things, but what do you do about it?" Her voice was bleached of all feeling.

Aghast, he gaped at her … did she really want to know or was she simply expressing her contempt. He was convinced that in her heart of hearts somewhere, she held him responsible for whatever had happened to her … and, to be truthful, he really was the one to be blamed. If he hadn't made her work … but then, in all fairness, she'd been working long before she'd got married.

He lapsed into the previous mode, "I just keep imagining all sorts of things, brooding, eating my heart out and desperately pacing around. I stand near the door waiting for you. But, I know it's silly. I know that there's nothing in my fears, that they're just my stupid imaginings. And so, that's why I do nothing."

Sheela sat up once again. It was as if she had washed away from her face the earlier look. But, nothing else had come to take its place – it was a blank, wooden face. She began, in an utterly indifferent voice, "I got off from work at 10 o'clock. By ten fifteen I was at the bus stop. Ten twenty, ten twenty-five, ten thirty – but my bus didn't come. The last bus must have gone past early, or it had been cancelled. I should have taken another bus. Not a single one was coming towards my side. I just kept standing. I could have taken a taxi or scooter, but I was too scared to travel alone at this hour." Sheela paused for a moment and tried to read the look on his face. Then, she continued, "at about 10.45 a bus showed up. I raised my hand. There was no board at the front. I had no idea where it was going. The bus stopped."

"It must have been going to the depot." He lit a cigarette and sat listening, attentively.

Sheela let him draw his cigarette and then spoke, "that's right! The conductor told me it was going to the depot. No problem, I told him, just let me off at Ring Road."

"There was no one else in the bus?" he asked suspiciously.

"No, there were two other guys," Sheela said.

"That was pretty brave of you." Reassured, he took a second pull at his cigarette.

"Yes," Sheela said, "but those two fellows got off at the next stop. When the bus started again, the conductor went to the driver and whispered something. I knew right then that they were up to some mischief. I realised then that I shouldn't have got on like this, into an empty bus."

His back peeling away from the sofa, he sat up bolt upright.

"Did they mess with you?" he blurted.

Sheela felt peeved. "What does it look like to you?"

He exploded, "I know those types! When they see a lone woman, they're bound to tease her. Our country, it's a disgrace how people's morals have gone to the dogs! Can't trust any bastard any more." Controlling himself, he changed his tone, "then what happened?"

"The driver switched off the lights in the bus."

"You didn't tell them not to?" He was pretty agitated.

"No." In that same flat voice, she said, "I was terrified. I couldn't utter a sound. I didn't want to provoke them by quarrelling with them. Just let me get home today, safe and sound. I'll go to the Hunuman Mandir, tomorrow, and make an offering, I thought."

He spoke teasingly, "that means we'll have to make a trip to the temple tomorrow, buy some prasad."

All her frustration, all her anger flashed onto her face, "so you think I've got home safe and sound?"

He felt very foolish. Sheela's fury was legitimate. He could only laugh sheepishly and leave it at that.

Sheela returned to that incident again. She seemed, somehow, to be totally detached from it all. She felt neither anger nor sorrow. Completely indifferent, as if all this had happened to someone else altogether, not to her at all. As if her part was simply to narrate this event. As if she was concerned only to describe the happenings in minute detail, and at great length. And, as she recounted the event, the details would rise from inside her and float away and be lost in the world outside…

"The driver put off the lights. The conductor, humming snatches from some silly romantic song, made his way to the back of the bus and sat down next to me. His insolence made me so mad, that I don't know where my fear vanished. I burst out, 'the whole bus is empty, can't you sit somewhere else'?"

A tremor passed right through him. "Did he get up?"

Her tone was still icy cold. "No chance! Get up? He just ignored what I was saying and shifted closer to me. Snuggling up right next to me, he asked, 'come baby! What's the problem'?"

Outraged, he stood up. He flung down his cigarette and crushed it under his shoe, "okay! Did you note the number of the bus?"

His indignation left Sheela cold. Almost seeming to pacify him, she said, "Yes! I've got the number all right, but just listen… it was pretty clear to me that it wouldn't stop at this. They were definitely going to do something or the other. I gave the conductor a real shove. He was taken completely by surprise and fell off the seat. I screamed loudly, "driver! Stop the bus!"

He stared at her numbly, while she, in her story-telling mode, carried on, "he didn't stop the bus. Actually, he speeded up."

"The road was deserted. Not a soul was around. I was alone in the bus, the lights were off and the bus was racing away."

"Then how did you get away?" he asked, swallowing the spit stuck in his throat.

"The conductor got up and lunged at me. I took off my sandal – I'd worn the steel stilettos today – and gave him a good thrashing. His face was full of scratches and bruises. Blood was trickling down his face."

"Good for you." He laughed a tense strangled little laugh. "If I'd just been there, I'd have beaten him good and proper."

She stared at him, the way an adult looks at a boastful child, "Yes, that's exactly what I thought. You'd have given him a good hiding, if you had been there. But, the pity is, they didn't give me the chance to come home and call you there. All I did was beat him as best as I could."

He lit his cigarette again. "That's good, that's good," he said.

"But he didn't let go. Then he caught hold of my blouse and pulled, and all the buttons just opened up with a single tug…"

"What?" His skin crawled, "give me that bus number. I'll do

something just now.... Horrible! How can any one live in this country. Not a single woman is safe here."

Sheela paid no attention to him. She carried on talking as though she would stop only when she finished telling him everything. "Seeing how deserted the place was, the driver had parked up the bus by then. Then the two got together. They stuffed a cloth into my mouth and tied up my hands..."

Outrage had left his throat parched and raw. Tears were pricking his eyes and Sheela sat there unmoved, as though she was narrating a story, not describing something that had happened to her.

"Even then, how did you escape?" he asked at last, in a strangled voice.

"How did I escape?" She laughed a peculiar sort of laugh. "Who said I escaped?" and laughing, she broke into tears. She realised now, for the first time, that all this had actually happened to her. And whatever had occurred had scarred her somewhere very deep inside, "the two of them, turn by turn ..." She covered her face with both her hands. She was sobbing uncontrollably.

He stood there stunned, an inanimate thing, as though everything had gone numb. Then, some faint sensation stirred beneath this cover of deadness. His heart was seething with anger but with it was mixed a deep fear. It took him a great deal of time to know, that everything which he had heard, had only filled him with terror, and the anger he felt was directed at Sheela alone.

"Why didn't you stop them? Why didn't you fight them off?" he screamed and asked.

Sheela stopped crying, suddenly. There was neither surprise nor grief in her eyes. In some corner of her mind, she had already suspected this. Her mind may not have accepted this reality, but she was aware at some deeper level, that her husband would never… perhaps she would have to fight him to convince him of her integrity… Exasperated, she asked,

"From everything that I have told you so far, what makes you think I didn't resist them enough?"

But her question did not affect his anger, "Before the driver walked back, the conductor was alone. Why couldn't you have jumped off the bus?"

Sheela's eyes gaped with disbelief, "you mean, I should have jumped from the racing bus? You were the one who told me everyday not to get off or get on to a moving bus… maybe you have no idea how fast the bus was going. Had I jumped, I would certainly have died. Nothing could have saved me."

He glared at Sheela, "wouldn't your dying been more admirable? How can you come home coolly and tell me that two men have… since you didn't die before, you should have died afterwards."

Sheela felt that somewhere, she had already been prepared for this conversation, for these allegations, for these insinuations. In an instant she flared up, "stop talking nonsense. Who are you to make all these charges? If two ruffians waylay you tomorrow and beat you up, break your arms and legs, gouge out your eyes or cut off your nose, I'll tell you exactly what you are telling me… Very heroic of you to worry so much about your wife's honour. If you're so infuriated, why don't you go and cut off their heads and bring them here?"

He began to tremble. What was she saying? How can he cut off anyone's head? The sight of blood terrified him. Hadn't he given up eating meat for this reason? How nauseated he felt.

"How can one do that. It's no longer…" He stopped. This wasn't an age of chivalry that he could go and cut off somebody's head. Then why was it that he thought that Sheela should be the one to die – "I can definitely report this to the police. Give me the bus number."

Sheela's tone turned ironical once again, "What will you tell the police – two men…"

He swung around sharply, "How can I describe such a thing?"

Sheela turned still more grave, "what else will you say? Two men molested your wife - you can't say a simple thing like this, and you want to kill me?"

"Who wants to kill you?"

Sheela said, "if I'd submitted willingly to all this you could have doubted my virtue, but the circumstances in which this happened gives you no right to cast aspersions on my character. Besides, even to preserve my honour, why should I die? I won't die! We'll live on like this. You don't tell anyone, and I won't tell anyone."

Without his knowing it, he felt completely weak. "I'm not fit to show my face to anyone. How can I face anyone…"

Sheela stared and then almost scolded, "why, what's happened to you? You haven't been raped. What's happened is with me. How does it affect you?"

This infuriated him. "You keep quiet! Another woman in your place would have killed herself by now, and you're joking."

"Listen! Whatever has happened doesn't make me feel good." She spoke calmly, "I feel no regret whatsoever because I'm not responsible for it. I refuse to die over this little business. As for you. You can hunt out those men and kill them if you want. You can report it to the police, if you like. And, if that doesn't work, you can abandon me…"

"I don't need you to give me advice, understand?" He had pulled himself out of his submissiveness. He had always had this grudge against Sheela. She'd never admit to her mistake and would begin to advise him instead. "You think that after all this has happened, we can carry on living like husband and wife! I live with you! People will point at me and say, 'this is the fellow whose wife was raped by a conductor and driver'. There was nothing left between us the moment you told me about this thing… snapped! Finished! You and I – there's an end to our relationship. You can't stay in my house anymore."

Sheela looked at him. He really was very angry. So angry that he could actually have pushed her out of the house. Perhaps he had nothing against those two men. All his discontent had descended onto Sheela. In truth, Sheela felt like laughing. But she didn't. Very patiently she said, "there's nothing between us. I won't live in your house. Anyhow, one concession I can make for you – if you can't remove your things tonight, you can have them picked up tomorrow morning. You might remember perhaps, this quarter is in my name."

He was stunned. That things would take this turn, he could never have imagined. He had completely forgotten about the quarter. It would have been much better if he'd thought about it earlier. The quarter was definitely Sheela's. She would live there. Most of the stuff would remain there too. At best, he'd carry his personal things. But where? Onto the road? The railway platform? He wouldn't be stupid enough to spend all his salary on two shabby little rooms in this atrociously expensive city. He wasn't even a government servant who could bank on an official quarter… then what? Stay in a hotel? At a friend's place? For how long?

He remained silent. Taking a deep breath, he continued to stroll back and forth… from one end of the room to the other. Soon enough, his breathing quietened and the clatter of his feet subsided. What he wanted to do was to laugh out loud and say, "let's forget all these silly things. Come, let's go to sleep."

But his ego, lurking within him, didn't allow him to laugh. Pacing around, he came and stood before Sheela, "I'll take my things tomorrow morning and go away." His nostrils flared, "get one thing very clear. You can't blackmail me like this, understand? Tomorrow, if I don't get the flush repaired you'll blackmail me, or if I can't kill the mouse in the store, you'll threaten me like this. If you have an affair with another man, then too you'll blackmail me..."

At this moment, Sheela felt she had cracked into two from within. One half of her genuinely wanted to make peace with him. She knew that like herself, her husband had also been split into two. And like her, only one half of him was putting up a fight, that too, superficially, as if biding time till he was forgiven.

All at once, she broke down, "how wretched I feel. Even if we patch up, what use is it! If we have children and they find out what had happened to their mother, won't they want to kill themselves. Oh God! All because of me! My poor husband, my poor children..."

His stubbornness melted away. Sheela, for the first time, had taken the blame upon herself. He saw how she sat there with head bowed, crying.

He went up to her. Soothingly he spoke, "now go to bed. It's very late. You're a model of Indian womanhood. You'll be an inspiration for others... an unarmed woman fighting off two beasts in the shape of men. Anyhow, you go off to sleep. You've had a long day and tomorrow you have to go to work again."

Sheela raised her head and wiped away her tears. "I'll go to bed. But you aren't leaving tomorrow with your things are you?"

"We'll think about that later. You go off to sleep," he said. "Just have a look at yourself in the mirror, you'll know then how worn out your poor face looks."

Bravely, Sheela tried to smile a little and playfully said, "No, first you tell me that you're not leaving tomorrow. I wouldn't be able to sleep for a moment otherwise. I'd be scared sick that from tomorrow I'll have to live alone in this quarter."

"You really do worry too much," he agreed, "okay, I'll not go. Besides, how would you fight the case all by yourself? You will have far too many problems living by yourself."

Sheela looked at him again – even now he was harping on the issue of the case. Some traces of ego still lingered, perhaps.

"Shall we go to sleep now?" she asked.

"Yes, come, let's sleep. I'm sleepy too," he said, and quietly went and lay down on his bed.

THE CURSE OF SALT

It began several months ago. It was neither permanent nor continuous. Quite at random, I felt breathless or felt my chest splitting apart. It usually occurred when I quickened my pace. I would then stop in my tracks or cautiously move my feet in measured steps. In a couple of minutes I would be normal again.

Sometimes I experienced the pain, even without walking fast. Whenever I had to catch a bus or a train, I would begin fretting: What if the bus left earlier, or the train is over crowded? The tension would somehow filter down from my mind to my chest. The sensation would be that of pins pricking all over, followed by a sharp pain and the feeling of my chest bursting apart. I would pant for breath as though I had just completed a cross-country run. There would be trouble in breathing as though my lungs were devoid of any air and yet were unable to absorb a fresh intake. It reminded me of a crowd trying to enter a train all at once. I felt as though I would faint or collapse but neither happened.

I happened to casually mention it to my daughter-in-law one day. My effort was to underplay it, but she was immediately worried. Nearly the whole day she hung around the balcony, waiting for my son. All she came in for was to serve me lunch and to check my well-being. The terrified look in her eyes and the bunched up end of her sari fisted in her palm made me feel as though she half expected to see my chest torn apart, or holes in it from end to end in which she would quickly stuff her pallu to clog them up. Tch, Tch. Poor thing, she never had the opportunity to do so.

When my son returned in the evening, she blabbered everything to him even while he was on the staircase. He came to my room and worriedly enquired about my well-being. When I described my pain to him, he was annoyed that I hadn't told him earlier. He left to call the doctor.

In fact, he called not one but many doctors. All of them examined me inside out, knocked me up, felt me all over and then concluded that I had no ailment. It was only my age that made me feel the way I did. They explained that advancing age had a debilitating effect on the nerves and any kind of mental or physical exhaustion and tension caused these painful bouts. Since there was no cure for old age, nothing could be done about my malady. Their prescription was - keep away from brooding tension and physical exhaustion.

I thought about it a lot when left alone. Do I really think so much? Do I worry, or tire myself? Raking my brains gave me a dull headache. I felt I never really had an opportunity to deliberately think or worry about something or systematically tire myself physically. I concluded that perhaps one doesn't wish it, but with age these things come naturally. I too couldn't find a cure for my condition.

That day I visited the market close to our home. I had run out of cigarettes, so I simply had to go. I couldn't expect my son or his wife to run this errand. I climbed down the stairs, looked carefully on either side before crossing the road to reach the shop. The shopkeeper immediately handed me a carton containing ten packs of Gold Flake, all neatly packed in a box of Panama, the moment he saw me. He knew me and my brand too well. 'Engineer sahib's father ...' was how all shop owners referred me as here. He also knew that I smoked none other than this brand and came into his shop for cigarettes only, as I never had *paan*. I always bought packs of ten together from him.

I made the payment and turned back. All of a sudden I felt the familiar creep into my chest accompanied by sweat-beads on my forehead and then my whole body was drenched in perspiration. I thought that the pain would subside in a couple of minutes, but it only intensified with time, like exhaled smoke from a cigarette dispersing gradually in the air.

I leaned on the counter of another shop and finally sat there. The shop owner recognised me and accompanied with a couple of more of his ilk, dropped me home.

My son was away at work and my daughter-in-law, who was alone, got very flustered. She made a call to the doctor immediately followed by another to my son's office. The doctor came within five minutes and my son soon after. He advised my son to shift me to a good hospital immediately. There was no time to lose, he felt as I had had a heart attack and could have a failure any moment.

My chest was ready to burst open and I too was puzzled as the pain had prolonged a bit too much. But this wasn't the first time. On other occasions, the pain had lasted a couple of minutes. No one had diagnosed it as heart trouble then. They had called it an old age complication. And now.... was it that one malady had different names or old age and heart trouble were synonyms for the same affliction?

The cab my son had come home in was waiting outside and I was bundled to the hospital in it.

My heart was sinking. I felt I was gradually losing my senses. I was mobbed by a group of doctors, who looked to me like an assortment of children gathered to watch a monkey or a bear perform antics. They were examining, touching and prodding me. Several machines were attached to my legs, arms and chest.

And just as I felt my chest would split open and I would die, they gave me an injection.

In the night, when it was time for all to sleep, I woke up and saw the doctor on his round. He told me that I was to be confined to my bed and had a special contraption put around it to prevent me from disobeying him. The pillow was taken away as I was to sleep without one. Sitting on the bed was absolutely prohibited - the advice was total bed rest. Even the diet prescribed was milk, that too skimmed. Salt, fat and cigarettes were barred.

I kept gaping at the doctor. I did not have a mirror, but I'm sure my mouth had fallen open in astonishment. Reading my thoughts, the doctor said in a consolatory tone, "Thank God, you reached the hospital in the nick of time. A delay of a couple of minutes could have cost you your life. God save you from a relapse now."

After he left, I couldn't sleep a wink. Won't these people allow me to use the toilet? They want me to lie down all the while and will give me a bed-pan. Ugh! How filthy can anyone be. These rascals, pretending to be clean, yet cannot differentiate between the toilet and the bed.

After three days of a diet of only milk, I retched. Skimmed milk was served three times a day. Apples and oranges came from home. I felt that I couldn't bear the sweet taste of milk. My palate was craving for something salty.

I felt quite ravenous. So much so that my intestines began rumbling agonisingly. But the appearance of the nurse with the customary glass of milk, killed my hunger instantaneously. Milk... more milk... I was nauseated.

It was only after a month that I was permitted to get down from my bed and use the toilet. I had never been so thrilled going to the loo. This made me hopeful of going home and tasting something salty.

The moment I stepped on the floor, my feet wobbled dangerously and I sat back. I scrutinised my body closely. I had grown extremely scrawny. My feet could not bear the burden of my thin lean frame.

I don't know what went on in my mind, but the moment I saw the doctor, I lost my cool. I felt like catching him by the scuff and slapping him hard. But my body did not budge. I spoke bitterly, "Keeping me on a starvation diet has made me so weak, that my feet cannot bear the burden of my own body. Do you want to kill me?"

The doctor looked at me dispassionately and replied, "You will gradually regain your strength." After a few days, I was able to take some steps leaning on my bed for support. I had watched my son first sit, then stand shakily when he was learning to walk. My grandson had learned to walk similarly, only a year ago. I would let him hold my finger and see him tread unsurely. I had come down to his level and was learning to walk again.

That day they served me rice and curds. My teeth had forgotten chewing. The exercise of masticating a couple of times made my jaw ache. I disliked the bland taste of rice and curds and now this confounded jaw ache. I gave up the exercise after a while and slipped my plate to the side.

The next day, I was in pain again. My chest was bursting and I was drenched in perspiration. My heart was sinking and the doctors mobbed me again. I also spotted my son and daughter-in-law in the crowd. My grandson was there too. The couple was crying and the child helplessly looked at his mother and then at his father.

The doctors felt that there had been some lapse in the abstinence diet and so I was back to the skimmed milk routine.

I couldn't sit up. Even the ordeal of getting up to swallow pills made me pant for breath.

Feigning a friendly tone, I whispered to the doctor, "Doc, why don't you kill me with some medicine, instead of starving me like this?"

The doctor burst out laughing. "We are on the right track. We are deliberately making you weak and melting away your fat," he said.

That evening when my son came to visit me, I pleaded to him, "Take me home."

"The doctor does not advise that," he replied.

"Don't let him, but you take me along," I reiterated.

"You are being treated here," he explained.

"These people are gradually killing me," I whispered in a conspitorial tone. "They are melting my fat, then they will melt my bones. They will not let me return home alive. You needn't come here every day. You can ask them when you've got to come to collect my body."

He was in tears. He held my hand in his. "Father please do not think like this," he pleaded. "You will be fine. They are treating you and you've got to understand. If I take you away against their wishes and you go through a similar bout again, they are not likely to readmit you. This is the only good hospital here. Small towns have a dearth of these." He went away.

I thought about it a lot and concluded that my son was not likely to agree to my viewpoint. He loved me too much and would like to treasure me as long as he could. Something I did with my grandfather's watch - carefully put it away in the almirah. It did not work, but it was just lying there.

When the doctor came in, someone from within me begged, "Doc, give me something to eat."

I did not recognise this person within me. Very pitiable. My grandson used to simper in a similar manner while asking his mother for a chocolate. But I was so old.

"What will you have?" the doctor asked me.

"I'm tired of drinking milk," I said and after that the stranger within me continued, "Doctor give me something salty. Okay, give me a spoonful of salt." The stranger's mouth began watering at the mere sound of the world salt.

"Salt is poison for you," he warned, "It cannot be given to you. A slice of plain bread and salt-less boiled vegetable is all that can be given."

Boiled papaya and beans. I couldn't have these even for two days. How on earth can anyone regard these as decent edible vegetables... that to without a trace of salt!

When my son came in the evening, I exploded with anger. "You don't want to take me home and want me to die here. They starve me. You want me to crave for every morsel before I die. I will turn into a ghost, a real ghost."

My son quitely watched me. And when I had cooled down after the monologue, he began describing his day at the office.

After he left, I became restive. I felt as if part of a rehearsal of a drama, full of hustle and bustle, where amidst shouting, repeated attempts were being made to enact a perfect role.

On seeing the doctor, the stranger within me was alert again. Folding my palms and assuming a very polite tone I said, "Doc, please have pity on me."

On the bend of the road leading to the station, I had often come across an old man sitting on a dirty cloth-piece. He had a long straggy beard, filthy mucous-eyes and saliva oozing out from either corners of his mouth. He used to touch his head in obeisance to the ground while whining, "Give me one paisa O' baba."

I felt as though the old man, dusting the dirt from his old cloth had stood up and found a place within me. The same old man told the doctor "Don't starve me to death. Give me something edible. I cannot eat this."

"Will you have fish?" the doctor enquired.

"Fish." The very suggestion brought saliva to my mouth! "O, yes doctor! Fish."

The doctor made a note on his pad and left me. I did the best to recall the taste of fish. It was ages since I had tasted it. I couldn't get the taste back into my mouth. But I knew it was delicious.

"What a hog I am," I tried to push the beggar from within me. If people find out how much I think about food, what will they think about me... What sort of father my son has? I was not able to sustain this thought for long. The thought of eating fish had started haunting my mind and that old beggar was once again comfortably seated within me. Sometimes the fish swam on the surface and sometimes was concealed in the layers below. Sometimes I could see its entire body and sometimes only the mouth. "Only if they could fry some fish pakoras," I thought to myself.

When the nurse wheeled in the food trolley and placed the fish on my plate, I was stunned. It was bland, white, boiled and salt-less - as good as raw.

I had read about sailors lost at sea compelled to have raw fish when they ran out of food supplies. But I... I tried to gulp a piece... then felt like asking the nurse to get me a tub of water; I'll rather make the fish float in that... I dreamt of a floating fish the whole night.

The next day there was a new nurse with the food trolley. I began preparing myself. If she was even slightly skeptical, then things would be messed up. But why should she be suspicious? I looked carefully on either side of my bed. No one was looking. I took the plate lying near the foot of my bed and hopped on to the adjacent bed. The patient from this bed had been discharged in the morning and that had set me thinking...

The nurse came near me, dragging the food trolley behind her and served me *chapatis*, salted boiled and mashed potatoes and spicy keema. The moment she moved ahead I slipped back to my bed. I did not touch the *chapatis*. I scooped a spoonful of keema into my mouth which had begun dripping with saliva. It was nearly two months since my tongue had tasted salt. And this had much more than that - a generous dash of spices.

Suddenly I had a slithering sensation of fear down my spine. If someone was to see the *keema* and salted potatoes on my plate, it would be snatched away. I felt as though there was a savage beast within me with sharp claws and fangs who was ready to tear open anyone. I was ready to kill anyone who dared snatch my plate.

By the time the new nurse finished her duty, she realised her mistake and I could see her fiddling with the papers in her hand. She turned and briskly walked to my bed and stood near it. The slimy lizard of fear that had been crawling on my spine, froze on my bone. I tightly clinched the plate in both my hands with all the strength I had in me.

But the nurse had moved beyond me; she wasn't snatching my plate. She was looking stunned at the chart behind me which clearly said 'boiled.' My grip on the plate eased a bit. I forced a smile on my face and whispered, "Sister, don't be scared, I shan't breathe a word to anyone." She came out of her stupor and reiterated "Please don't tell anyone... please." I nodded my head in agreement and she left.

Now I was in no hurry. I looked at my plate. The *keema* was over. I was enjoying the salted mashed potatoes. I recalled in my childhood while having a chocolate, I used to just keep a bit in my mouth when I realised that it would be over soon. As the mashed potatoes were on the verge of getting over, I began to scoop less and less on the spoon and prolonged the pleasure of eating it.

Today I had smiled after many days. I felt like laughing aloud, running in the ward and screaming to the doctors, "All of you are insane."

In the evening, the regular nurse was on duty again. She came with the trolley and dumped boiled beans and several pieces of boiled fish on my plate.

"Sister please," I pleaded. I felt as though the stranger within me had merged with my persona and the two of us could not be separated.

"Sister a bit of *keema*, for the change to my taste buds."

"Oh no, not for you," she said pulling the trolley ahead.

Exercising great restrain, I prevented myself from throwing the plate at her.

I had two new patients on either side of my bed now. In fact, I had struck a good acquaintance with one to my right and my mind had been working on a plan ever since.

After the nurse left, I exclaimed loudly, "So many things". I observed that the patient on my left heard me and was looking at my plate. "Would you like to have some fish," I endearingly asked him with the best of my smiles. Before he could mumble a reply, I got up from my bed and emptied three or four pieces of fish on his plate.

"O, why did you do this," he said, "what will you have now?"

"I have enough left here," I said.

He did not heed and forcibly emptied a lot of cauliflower on to my plate.

The cauliflower - a deep shade of yellow on account of the seasoning with the turmeric and spices - was on my plate. I slurped my tongue hungrily and swallowed it all. I felt like literally falling at the feet of my neighbour and requesting him to give me some of his vegetable everyday.

That same evening my son took me home. At home, he told me that the doctors had been thinking of discharging me for a long time but hadn't told me fearing that I would pester him to expedite it.

I was happy to be home. At least I was free of the nagging staff. Even a slight delay in lying back on the bed after having my medicines would elicit a sharp order to comply, from the sister-in-charge on the other end.

At home when I was served bland, boiled and salt-less vegetables for lunch, my temper rose and I threw the plate. It clanged noisily on the floor before breaking into pieces, scattering all the vegetables. I saw my daughter-in-law, pressing a section of her left foot. Probably a piece of china had pierced her. But I did not relent. I was so angry that had she been someone else, I would have thrown the pieces of china or any other thing I could get hold of, at her.

"If you wanted to give me this food why bring me home," I shouted, and lay down trembling with rage. She did not say a word and called my son instead. Seeing him, I sat up again and he simply stared silently at me. I continued my tirade, "Instead of leading a life of starvation, it is better to eat, drink and die," I said.

"O father, try and understand our predicament," he answered with tears in his eyes, "How can we give you poison?"

They left my room without giving me an opportunity to say anything. I lay down in a fitful mood.

The maid cleared the room and my daughter-in-law served me food once again. This time on a steel plate so that I wouldn't break it.

I realised that my son and my daughter-in-law were determined not to budge from their stand. My temper, any amount of bullying would not serve any purpose. "Friend...," I said to myself, "Use your brains..."

The next day, after my son had left for his work and my daughter-in-law was busy reading in her room, I called my grandson on the pretext of playing with him. My grandson had not met me during my stay at the hospital. He came to me with great longing.

"Who wants to have a chocolate?" I said taking him in my lap.

"Babloo," he replied.

"Then, dear Babloo, must run to the kitchen and fetch me some salt." I put him down on the floor.

I had my doubts how this three-year old could get hold of salt, but there was no harm in trying. I waited for him to return.

He came in with a pinch of salt in his tiny palm. With great efforts, I retrieved it and then licked his palm greedily. I licked almost all the salt he gave me with my fingers and whatever little was left, I wrapped up in a bit of paper and hid it under my pillow.

"Babloo, where did you get this salt from," I enquired.

"Meena gave it to me," he said.

Meena was the maid.

This wasn't a bad modus operandi, it could work after all. I began thinking - If I could bribe her with a couple of rupees, she might give me salty food and cigarettes too - perhaps. Cigarettes....

"Chocolate," Babloo reminded me.

"Your papa will get them from the market in the evening," I said bundling him out of my room.

My mind was preoccupied with a longing for cigarettes.

Babloo left the room in a sulk. He never expected me to cheat him.

"Cigarettes", I thought. "The day they took me to the hospital, I had bought a carton containing the Gold Flake packs. They should be in my almirah."

I locked my room and opened the almirah. All the ten packs were lying right in front. Matchsticks too. I took a pack out and my cupboard which was forever open was locked up and the keys safely put away in my pocket. My son couldn't snatch my cigarettes....

In the evening I was smoking one when I heard my son come up to my room. I immediately snuffed it out... Suddenly a bulb flashed in my mind... I re-lighted the cigarette and relaxing against the wall began puffing at it. He came to the door, drew the curtain aside. "How are you Fath...?"

He saw the cigarette, snatched it and put it out.

"Where did you get this from," he indignantly asked.

It did not take much effort. I comfortably said, "Your wife brought them for me."

It wasn't difficult to lie anymore. I had practiced it for long.

My son left immediately. I sat in my room listening to the quarrelling voices of the couple. He was hollering and she was soft at first and gradually she got louder and more strident. She was denying something repeatedly. And then I heard him slap her. Everything was still after that.

Lying on my cot, I smiled to myself. I knew my daughter-in-law too well. From tomorrow I could expect salt n' spice, vegetables and cigarettes too.

"My son is a first class fool." I thought to myself.

SHUTTLE

Shuffling about the room, Ishardas once again sat down on his charpoy. Propped up against the wall, pillow behind his back, he sat on this charpoy all day, reading something or the other.

Even when he had a job of his own, then too he had to read. But then time was short and books were in plenty. He'd go to the bazaar and buy books and magazines as he pleased. Whenever he was free, he'd sit down to read. How many times his wife, Bhagwanti, would have to call him before he'd come to the kitchen to eat! And as he ate, the book would be in his hand. Bhagwanti wasn't educated nor had she any interest in books. A simple rustic girl, silent and reserved; she was now less of a girl and more of a woman.

Once in a while Bhagwanti did get irritated. "Can't you eat in peace, the book won't vanish, will it!" she'd chide and snatch the book from him.

Ishardas wouldn't resist. He knew it was only the two of them at home. If he were to read what was she to do on her own? A quiet sort of woman, she didn't go about much in the neighbourhood. He wanted to dispel her loneliness but Bhagwanti's quiet temperament didn't encourage him to chat much with her either.

And in the end, they'd get around to talking of books. Whatever he happened to be reading, he'd read it aloud for her. Thereafter, Bhagwanti had no objection to books anymore. She began to prefer her husband's books to the meddling chatter of the neighbourhood women.

But ever since his failing health had compelled him to retire he'd begun to feel extremely lonely. Plenty of books were still bought but they were chosen by his sons. What a difference between his taste and their's! His sons read romances and Ishardas positively disliked them.

Then his sons got married. Modish magazines took the place of novels. Women's magazines, of what use were they to him? And when their children were old enough to read and 'Chandamama' and 'Balbharti' were bought, what would he do then?

Even today he had nothing to read. There was nothing else for him to do either. Bhagwanti had gone away to their eldest son's place. The eldest bahu wasn't well and he had come and fetched his mother away.

Ishardas at times felt furious with his sons. As soon as one of them got married and a kid or two came along, he wanted to break away from his father and set up home on his own. But the trouble was that once on their own, they weren't prepared to contribute anything towards their parents. They'd say that with their own set-up how could they spare anything for their father. Yes, if they moved in with them, then they'd bear the cost.

To hell with bearing the cost - Ishardas would brood - one who'd been independent all his life and held his head high, he'd go beg food at his son's door! Ishardas would rather die of starvation than be dependent. If you can't give me anything, don't; who expects anything from you in any case?

He knew exactly what his sons really meant. No one actually wanted him to stay with them. Why would they want to keep him when he'd either lie around on his charpoy all day or struggle all day to read the printed pages before him.

What they really wanted was that their mother, Bhagwanti, live with them. Mind their children. Cook food for them. When they felt like going out, take care of the house. Wretches, want to be stylish! Kills them to get their wives to work. If they're all that fancy why don't they keep a servant, an ayah! That they will never do. What they'd like was to get for the price of feeding their mother, a cheap reliable maid servant.

Or else, one of the younger brothers or sisters could go stay with them. Who'd run around like errand boys to fetch things form the bazaar for them. Or hand to their memsahib's, lolling on the charpoy, their glasses of water or cups of tea. And, take aside their children and divert them so that their parents could go out when they felt like.

There was no way Ishardas would settle for any such arrangement. That his wife or children should work to support him was in any case unacceptable to him. Should things come to such a sorry state then it were better they serve in a stranger's house where they could at least demand their rightful wages.

But occasionally, when either of the two elder sons showed up whining that his wife was seriously ill and things at home were an absolute mess, then Bhagwanti just had to go. At such moments, the paternal instinct hidden somewhere within Ishardas would surface and he himself would urge Bhagwanti to go, "why don't you go? When else will we be of use? What sort of a mother, are you? Don't want to help your sons when they need?"

Bhagwanti, cursing him, herself, her sons and their wives, would go. Left behind, Ishardas would pace about his room, puffing at his cigarette and staring at the road outside his window.

Ishardas knew that he'd now truly aged. Barring life's basic needs, he had nothing in common with his children any more. For them, he was just another worthless object lying about the house, which from long habit or fear of public condemnation, they couldn't even throw away.

Not one of his sons wanted to sit with him for even five minutes. They'd sit whispering outside his door and then one would enter and inform him if there was anything of importance. They'd never really come to him. It was Ishardas who'd sometimes join his sons, but one by one they'd slink away and ultimately Ishardas would be alone again.

It was Bhagwanti alone with whom he could talk once in a while. She was the only one who could comprehend what he had to say. She belonged to the same era as Ishardas, but even she had little time. After all she wasn't as useless as he was, a hundred chores waited for her in the kitchen or bathroom. Otherwise, she had to dust and tidy up the house.

She was still a part of the domestic mainstream. Not like Ishardas, sitting on the water's edge, like a lifeless stone. Every member of the family was linked to her by some need or the other. May be it was only because she did their tasks but then she was still a part of them.

But when she rested in the afternoon or by evening, she lay exhausted on her charpoy in the courtyard, then Ishardas would come and sit by her. Thirty five years they'd been together. Bhagwanti alone could understand him. Together they'd built up this home. Borne these children. Raised them. Educated them. Married off three of them. Soon, the fourth would be married too. The eldest two had shifted out and he knew that the third was busy dreaming of moving away as well. Huddled together in their room, what else could husband and wife be talking of?

And when Bhagwanti goes away to the eldest son's place there's not a soul left in the house who'd exchange even a word with him. This loneliness bothered Ishardas deeply. He wondered often — these sons married just for a couple of years, why couldn't they realise that it had been thirty five years their parents had been married.

These wretches couldn't live away from their wives for a day, then how could he, so utterly dependent these last thirty five years, live without Bhagwanti. Not one was prepared to spend even a minute with him in his old age and they were bent on taking from him, his companion of thirty five years.

Just the other day, Bhagwanti was away at the other son's place. After a week, she'd come home to see him saying "she'd check out how their father was doing". What a commotion there'd been at home! All of them going about the house with smirks on their faces. These wretches think these old people have gone senile. If for nothing else, shouldn't they have made some allowance for the friendship that had grown out of their thirty five-year-long association! But no! They thought only their marriages have been made in heaven. How could anyone else have any attachment at all!

It isn't just the loneliness when Bhagwanti is away, there are a hundred other problems for Ishardas. He never gets his tea on time in the morning. Once she's given her husband his tea, the daughter-in-law thinks no one else needs anything. On the other hand, Bhagwanti calls him into the kitchen and makes sure he's eaten properly before serving anyone else. She knows exactly what doesn't suit him, how much salt he likes, how much masala. But no, bahu can't call him into the kitchen and serve him there. She brings his thaali and hands it to him there right on his charpoy. And then, sometimes she forgets to give him the water, at other times, the roti. Sometimes there's not enough vegetables. sometimes too little salt and masala in the dal. He silently eats what he is given. When he's eaten two rotis, he sits around for five minutes hoping that someone might come with a roti. Or if he runs out of vegetables, he waits but when no one comes, he picks up his thaali and leaves it in the kitchen. Then bahu remembers – "Babuji ! Sabzi ! babuji, roti......"

"No child!" he says, "it's okay, I've finished."

When he bathes, no one bothers that his clothes are dirty, that he be given fresh ones. He doesn't even know where his clothes are kept. For thirty five years he's had no idea about his clothes. Bhagwanti's taken care of all that. When he goes to bathe, his clothes are already hung up in the bathroom. Now that Bhagwanti is away looking after one of her bahus, he goes around in dirty clothes for days on end.....

So many little things of this sort. Can't ask for anything. When Bhagwanti's here he doesn't need to ask. She knows exactly what he needs and when. And, should he need to ask where's the hesitation in asking one's wife! When his wife controls the home he too has a right on everything there. But the minute Bhagwanti leaves, the home become alien. He can't ask his bahu for anything and none of them knows what his needs are. Nor do any of them want to know ....

Now today it's exactly ten days that Bhagwanti left. For ten days, non-stop he's been pacing about in this fashion. Smoking cigarette after cigarette and staring out of the window. In these ten days, except to ask him for food no one has spoken to him at all. Like any household pet he's been getting his food at the right time – and that's all. That he also needs company, also dislikes loneliness – no one has even given it a thought. In these ten days, not once has he eaten a decent meal. And in these ten days he's changed his clothes only once.....

For how long can he carry on in this way! God knows how long the elder bahu remains sick. Who knows if they want her to get well at all. How can he survive stifled like this. He feels that someone has locked his room from the outside. Not a room anymore it's become a cage. And everyday that cage is shrinking and he's choking in it. He can't bear this suffocation anymore.

Then why not go to the elder son's place for a while. Surely, as a father-in-law, he should enquire after the bahu's health. When his daughter's sick, doesn't he go visit her? Where's the difference between a bahu and a daughter. And then Bhagwanti's there. He'll spend a little time with her. Wonder how she is. Poor woman, pity she has to slog this hard in her old age. He can even play with his grandchild for a while.

So many things for him to do there, it now seems necessary for him to go. Ishardas had already planned out everything. He wanted to get up right away and set off. But he must tell someone here before going. Here at this hour who'd he tell he wanted to go to his elder son's?

Wonder if there's anyone at home or not. Bahu would be there, of course, but where would he look for her. Could be in the kitchen or her room, the bathroom or the courtyard. That'd be tedious. Besides, it didn't seem proper to tell bahu and push off. He knew that afterwards they'd all sit and laugh at him and find it awfully funny.

Better to wait till afternoon. Whoever came to give him lunch he'd say he wanted to go to the elder son's in the evening or rather he was going. Yes, it's better, he'd say definitely that he was going. Each of them would have his say. Well, let them. There'd be ample time between the announcement of his plan and his departure. Enough time to know their reaction. It'd be best for him to wait, he decided.

When bahu came with the *thaali* at lunch time, he said softly, "Bahu ! I'm going to Bade's house this evening! If there's anything I can do there, let me know."

"No ! there's nothing to be done," she said and briskly left the room.

She'd go tell her husband - Ishardas knows - and they'll tell the rest of them. They'd all smirk knowingly at one another and say, "without Amma Babu ji feels lost even now."

But he wouldn't care. Why bother about those who aren't willing to use their brains. He knows that they've given up thinking of him as a human being....

In a while their third son showed up, "Babuji ! Believe you're going to meet Amma!"

Something shrunk deep within Ishardas - to meet Amma! Yes, he was going to meet her. "Yes! I'm going to Bade's place. I'll find out how bahu's doing," he acknowledged in different words.

"When will you go?" his son asked.

"When it cools off a bit by evening, I'll go." What was the relevance of all these questions, he couldn't see. He'll go whenever. What was the need for all this cross examination?

This third son had perhaps gauged his feelings. "It'll take you pretty long to reach," he said, "and then, naturally, you'll want to stay for a while and before you know, it'll be dark !" He paused before suggesting, "why not stay for the night? You can return tomorrow morning."

Overnight! Not a bad idea - Ishardas mused. That way he'd get some extra time there. "But I'm only going to find out how bahu is," he said.

"That's okay," his son said, "but what's the big hurry! Why not take it easy and go and come leisurely. After all, that's also like home, isn't it?"

No denying this. But baggage? He'd definitely need a couple of things.

"Should I get your things packed?"

And he left the room before Ishardas could answer.

Shortly afterwards bahu had placed a bag by him.

What would bahu have packed he wondered, perhaps some clothes. His shaving things, datun. She knows he uses only neem datun. He may not find that at Bade's place. They're all fancy folk there – all of them use toothpaste, no one's for datun.

What else might she have packed ? If Bhagwanti had put his stuff together, everything he needed would be there in one bag. But if Bhagwanti had been around, he wouldn't have needed to go anywhere at all. But then, it's all right. He'd manage. It must be okay. Anyhow, he wasn't travelling to an alien land, only to Bade's place. Besides, that was home too. He'd get whatever he needed there as well.

Not a bad idea staying over. Good suggestion the third son had given. The eldest often grumbled that he had never come to stay with them. He'd also be satisfied.

Ishardas had set off by late afternoon and was at Bade's before evening.

His son was not back from office yet but Bhagwanti and bahu were at home. When he asked her, bahu told him she still felt awfully weak. Could have a relapse any time.

But it was Bhagwanti's health Ishardas should enquire about, not bahu's. He knew that bahu wasn't well and that Bhagwanti was here to help her out. But to him bahu seemed well enough; it was Bhagwanti who looked ill. Very run down and positively weak.

"How are you," he asked sitting down on the edge of her charpoy after considerable hesitation.

"I am okay," Bhagwanti moistened her lips with her tongue and spoke in a faint voice. She shifted aside, "sit properly!"

Ishardas settled down comfortably. Who'd know Bhagwanti as thoroughly as he did. This shrunken face, licking her lips repeatedly, speaking slowly as if she needed all her energy simply to speak. It was clear to him she wasn't well at all. When she's alright she's not this sluggish. She's not lethargic by nature.

"How's everyone at home?" Bhagwanti asked.

And bit by bit he gave her a report on each one. And he told her about himself, how everything was fine with him and what good care the third bahu took of him. No problem of any sort at all for him.

He kept on telling her, looking at her face all the while. It was clear to him that Bhagwanti knew he was lying. Bhagwanti knew him and her bahus far too well. But then neither of them was in the habit of complaining.

A deep pool of resentment against his eldest son was building up inside Ishardas. Can't he see his mother's state. Doesn't he know how much she has to slog. If his wife's little finger so much as hurts he sheds tears but he doesn't even notice his mother as she lies exhausted on her bed. His wife's simply glowing with health and here's this poor old woman, not a drop of blood in her, but still working to the bone.

He was angry too with Bhagwanti. Where's the need for her to kill herself for them. Want to live on their own, then let them manage their wives and kids. Let her work if she wants to but why slog like this for them.

He wanted to tell Bhagwanti, "Come up! Get ready, I'm taking you home with me. No need to kill yourself here." But he knew that Bhagwanti would never leave this way nor would it be proper to take her away so. Bada would be really upset and Ishardas didn't want to irritate anyone.

He heard the knock at the door and then his grandson exulting, "Papa ! Papa! Papa's come."

His son was back.

He got up from the charpoy - better go meet his son. He'd go meet his wife first, ask her how things were. She'd tell him about Ishardas then he'd come over to meet them.

Ishardas and Bhagwanti both sat silently. He waited and wondered when his son would come over. Perhaps Bhagwanti was wondering too.

"Namaste, Babuji."

"Bless you," Ishardas said, "how are you?"

"What can I say," he'd sat down too, "lot's of hassles. Somehow she's not getting well at all and here Amma's also out of sorts. I really don't know what to do."

Ishardas sat silent. What should be say?

"And how are you?"

"I'm alright", Ishardas said, "quite comfortable."

"What's in the bag?" and not waiting for a reply he carried on, "I've told you so many times Babu ji you mustn't bother to bring anything. You always bring something or the other when you come…."

"I haven't brought anything, son," Ishardas said, "they're my clothes."

"Oh !" he laughed, "I am just coming."

And he walked off.

Ishardas felt a little guilty. Why hadn't he brought anything? Was it proper to arrive empty handed…but how could he have brought? Did he have any money of his own? His sons have enough expenses of their own. They hardly gave a thing. Wasn't it enough that he is fed. If sometimes they'd give him some cash then…..

He'd told his son that he'd brought his clothes, but his son hadn't said anything. Wonder why he hadn't …

"When did you come, Babu ji?" His son was back.

"Must be an hour," he said, "been waiting for you, hadn't seen you for a long time. I'll make a move now."

"I've been wanting to come over myself," his son said, "but I think you'd better set off before it's dark, otherwise you'll find it difficult."

"Yes, you're right," Ishardas stood up. "Best to get home in good time."

"Come, I'll walk you to the bus stop," said his son.

"No, no, you relax." Ishardas picked up his bag, "You've just got home from the office. Must be tired. Besides, bahu is alone."

He turned, "Okay Bhago!"

It was ages since he'd called Bhagwanti by her pet name.

His son saw him off to the door.

"Babuji, this...." his son was giving him a rupee note, "for the bus."

Ishardas had an overwhelming desire to jangle his pockets and say, "I've plenty of money, son!"

But he silently took the note. Next time he'd bring something for the child.

"Okay, then..." and he set off.

Poor Bhago - he mused - if I'd stayed back she'd only have had more to do - one additional burden. Just as well his son didn't ask him to stay.

On the way he bought a pack of cigarettes with his son's note. Once home he'd be stuck in his room smoking cigarette after cigarette - Who'd go - he mused - to fetch him more.

He lit up a cigarette and made his way slowly to the bus stand. The bag, a needless burden, in his other hand.

THE FLAT DOWNSTAIRS

She lay in the darkness staring fixedly at the ceiling. She was not in fact seeing anything at all, it was just that her eyes were open. It was as though the entire power of her senses had been gathered somehow into her ears. Her only effort was to make out that sound; was there any sound at all or was she simply imagining?

Suddenly, her gaping eyes opened wider still, but the vacant look in them had changed. In those hitherto expressionless eyes, there was now a definite emotion. It was fear. Fear had loosened the tense lines on her face and seemed in an instant to disfigure them. Even in the darkness her face appeared to change colour, fading towards a sickly yellow. After a considerable effort she wet her lips with the tip of her tongue and noiselessly turned onto her side. Very gently she touched her husband, but her touch had no effect on him. Using all her strength she began to dig her nails into her husband's arm.

His eyes flew open. There was a questioning look in those eyes, but may be he had not yet comprehended why he had awakened. They were indeed open but his face gave no indication that he was awake.

Silently she whispered, "listen, I think I hear a sound from downstairs."

Instantly, he turned his ears below. Like her, his blank face took on a strained look that clearly confirmed that now he was fully awake. But almost as swiftly, all trace of anxiety was wiped from his face.

"There's nothing at all," he said and turned over. She stared silently, passively at her husband for a while, but was soon overcome by some deep fear that seemed to terrorise her. The confidence that waking her husband had given her, the relaxed look, all just vanished in an instant, like the light fading from a bulb that suddenly fuses. She was even more fearful now than she had been before. He would turn over and sleep off in an instant, and she would be wide-awake and as utterly alone as she had been before. Irritation now flowed and blended with the fear in her mind. Her husband was right there next to her, then why should she have to tremble and be panic-stricken?

Firmly, she shook him again. Annoyance had replace fear in her voice, "I'm telling you, there is someone down there. You think they will run away because you turn over and go back to sleep?" Her husband turned over and looked at her.

"You're definitely mistaken. Just because you're scared you can't get to sleep, and you won't let me sleep either. You are only imagining things."

But his voice was no longer free from anxiety. She sensed that he no longer believed a single word of what he was saying. "Why don't you go and take a look anyway," she said

He made no move to get up and lay just as he was, "if there is someone, he's down there in the flat below, isn't he, he hasn't broken into your house. You just lie quietly and go back to sleep, okay?"

She could sense that anger at her husband was steadily replacing her fear of being robbed. She pulled herself together lest she scream out loud. God knows whether a thief had actually got into the flat downstairs. It could simply be that one of the neighbours down there wasn't able to sleep. If she spoke even a little sharply, in this deathly silence, her voice would travel well beyond the walls of their room. The neighbours might actually think that they, husband and wife, carried on squabbling even at this unearthly hour.

She had heard plenty of things about this flat from her neighbours already. Everyone believed that any couple that moved into this flat would end up fighting. So far they had escaped. Why then should she scream in the dead of night and ruin this impression? First thing in the morning, the women would go around gossiping that the two of them had fought at night.

But then, how could she deny that there was a sound downstairs. It was most probably the cupboard being opened. Yes, the sound was definitely coming from the room at the back downstairs, the room in which they had placed their large steel cupboard. Mrs. Chand from downstairs had told her that when they had shifted last time, the cupboard had got stuck in the staircase. That was when it had got a small dent, and now every time you opened or closed it, the door would make this grating noise.

This was exactly the sound she could hear, as if somebody had opened that cupboard. What could be the need for them to open the cupboard at this late hour. Could it be that they had threatened Mr. Chand with a knife or gun and snatching the keys from him, were busy emptying it out?...

Involuntarily her hand again landed on her husband's arm, "listen! Someone has just opened the cupboard downstairs! Do go once and take a look!"

Her husband didn't even turn to look at her. He lay still exactly as he was. "If someone opens his cupboard in his own house, is it necessary for me to go and take a look?"

"Why would anyone open a cupboard at this hour?" she asked, her voice taking on a sharper tone.

"Look," and he turned towards her, "you're an intelligent, capable woman. You have a career of your own and like any professional you manage your life as well as any man or woman. Then you had better give up these silly womanish ways. This isn't at all how an educated intellectual behaves!"

"What is that supposed to mean?" she asked, her brow knitted questioningly.

"Don't you feel," he said, "that it really is silly to interfere in other people's affairs and know every single detail of their lives? Why or when someone opens the cupboard in his house, is that really any business of yours? Besides, correct me if I am wrong, as far as I know the cupboard manufacturers' union or the residents' association hasn't made any rule that owners must not open their cupboards after ten at night."

She felt foolish. Her husband had once again put his finger on her weakness, she was sincerely conscious of this fact. In spite of her every effort, she would do something or the other that would give her husband the opportunity to tell her how irrational she was. She was really annoyed with herself. After all, what stopped her from being genuinely modern? Why was she unable to stay aloof from those around her? If thieves had broken into the flat downstairs, what was it to her? They hadn't got to her house yet, then why like the old-time women did she pry into everyone's affairs.

Just then she heard from downstairs, a woman's scream, throttled, strangled, firmly muffled... she sat up in dread.

She looked towards her husband. He still lay there with his back to her. With both her hands, she gripped his arm and pulled him towards her with all her might. He was wide-awake, his eyes wide with terror, his face ashen, drained of all colour, as if the blood had been sucked from his body.

So, he had also heard the scream! Were there actually thieves downstairs? Surely she was right. Something dreadful was happening downstairs. They may have murdered someone, or perhaps Mr.Chand's pretty young daughter, Ratna…

"Do get up and see," she told her husband in a hushed and frightened tone.

But he continued to stare at her with those same terror-struck eyes. Then he stammered, "It may just be one of their private quarrels."

"Still, just take a look," she whispered once again

"Suppose," he swallowed the spittle that had gathered in his mouth, "thieves are actually there. Will I go and grapple with them? How would you like it if people read in the papers tomorrow," he said, getting truly worked up, "that a professor sahib was found involved in a scuffle with the town's leading ruffians? You know, we have to maintain our reputation. Our profession has its own dignity, I can't cheapen myself that much."

She realised there was an incongruity between the words he was uttering and the expression on his face.

Passive, inanimate, she sat staring into the dark. Deep within her, the vague indeterminate conjectures were beginning to take a definite form.

No … it was not merely her imagination, without a doubt something was going on downstairs and whatever it was, it was neither normal nor simple… and a knot began to form in the deepest layers of her stomach, becoming a writhing, wrenching pain.

From the deathly silence below, a low whimpering arose, so gentle, so soft it barely penetrated the stillness, merely nudging it in the hope of rolling it aside, and then may be, a male voice barely audible as though gently explaining, consoling…

Her husband looked at her. He was going to speak again at length, to say, "Look, the world is full of all sorts of people. Every possible kind of thing is happening all the time. What can we do about them? If we come through with our own reputation intact, we should be grateful. Decent people stay away from such things, they dodge and steer clear. Do you think that others will come to our help if the intruders get into our home...?"

She looked up and fixed her gaze upon her husband. He was saying, "in this brotherhood of third rate countries, our country too somehow manages to survive. Whatever other's may do, this is the only right way. Tell me what other possible way is there...."

"What if the people get into our house too?" she asked, "breaking the drawing room glass windows and getting in isn't difficult at all. They can easily get to us..." her throat was as dry as sandpaper. "We don't know how many they are. They could have knives with them, guns too... all this has become so common these days."

The expressions gathering on his face were those that unfailingly appeared whenever she said something he didn't like. She fell silent at once. It seemed as though he might cry any minute, he shrieked tearfully, "what's the use of speaking such nonsense at this time? If knives and guns have become common in Delhi, is it my fault? You think I am the Police Commissioner or something. You are much more to blame for the government's incompetence than I am. At election time, I told you not to vote for this party. But do you ever listen to anything I say?"

"You're an odd man." Her frustration burst out in spite of her best efforts, "whenever there is any trouble you start quarrelling with me. Everything is my fault! If the government is worthless and the police corrupt, it's because of me! If thieves have got into the flat downstairs, was I the one to go and call them. If those people come into our house then again I will be the one to blame."

"If not your fault then will it be mine?" He sat up so aggressively it seemed he would slap her. "When I told you we will put grills in the glass window and wooden doors, you were the one to say no. At that time you were obsessed with the look of the house. Why didn't you realise then that anyone, armed with knives and guns, could break in at night? Amazed, she looked helplessly at him. He was right, she was the one to oppose grills, but that was a different issue. This was just his old familiar habit.

"Okay, I did refuse, but why did you agree? The issue isn't the grills at all, it's just that you are waiting for an opportunity to scold me," she said.

"Yesterday, when you scolded me in the market was there a proper reason for it?" Suddenly they both fell silent. There was again some disturbance below, the sound of people coming out of the flat. Then someone seemed to have touched the door leading upstairs, even pushed at it.

They both stared at each other.

"We should go back to sleep," her husband said.

"Will they also come upstairs?" She spoke in a muffled voice.

"I don't know." He wiped the water from his eyes. A sour, foul tasting liquid was gathering in his mouth. He wished he could allow himself to weep loudly.

His wife had stood up. She crossed her arms tightly across her chest.

"What shall I do? What shall I do?" And she started to wring her hands desperately. Her voice had cracked and she had begun to cry. She wanted her husband to take her head in his lap and caress it gently. But he was doing nothing at all.

He kept on weeping, and he lost his temper, "why don't you come and lie down! If you go on like this, won't they find out that we are awake?"

"They will come, they will come!" and throwing up her arms she began to cry again.

"Go and lie down," he shouted, "so what if they do come? Let them take away whatever they like. What great treasure do we have here anyhow?"

"Who says there's nothing of value," she spoke in a hoarse voice. "Just today I brought home my pay, there's a good five hundred in the home. And you won't even try to stop them."

He was furious once again, "I've known for a long time that your money is a lot more precious to you than I am. You know that those fellows are well armed but you want me to go and fight them for your measly five hundred. You'd actually like me to lay down my life for this silly amount."

This had no effect on her. She carried on crying, "who's asking you to die. But I've been trying to wake you for such a long time. If you had got up by now, you could have called the police."

"Police!" He wrinkled his nose disgustedly. "As if they would ever have let me get to the police. As for the police, they would definitely be in league with them." He was silent as though his throat had become parched.

The pressure on the staircase door had begun to increase.

She looked at him. There was now no reproach on their faces.

She came quietly and lay down by his side.

"What'll happen now?" she asked.

"Nothing will happen," he said. "Just lie silently as if you are asleep, no matter what they take. We can't throw away our lives just for a few things. We're earning more then enough, we'll soon get plenty more."

"But... if ... if ..." and once again her throat tightened, "if they molest me?"

For a stunned moment he was silent.

"No, they won't trouble you," very softly he said, "you're not that young any more."

"But if they still molest me, then?" she was petrified.

"Then what," in a highly philosophic tone he said, "what can anyone do. What is destined to happen is bound to happen. There is no sense at all in throwing away one's life over it."

"Yes, I don't want to die yet!" she snuggled close to him.

"Yes," he remarked serenely, "after all Mr. Chand will also cover up the entire episode!"

TO START ONCE AGAIN

Since last evening, Ghanshyamdas had been quite unwell. Maybe, if things had been different, he wouldn't have stirred from his *charpoy.* He would have stayed quietly in bed. That was one of the blessings of having retired – no compulsion to get up for office any more. But there seemed little chance for him to lie around quietly today.

Calling out loudly, he suddenly said, "Can you hear me! You'd better pack a couple of *datuns* for me. We've no idea if we'll get any there or not."

Panting for breath, he fell silent. He just couldn't speak and shout too much any longer. All that had been happening since last night wasn't at all good for a heart patient like him. And, he would keep on brooding and a stabbing pain from under his left ribs would begin to travel upwards...

No one answered him. He didn't particularly want one, actually. He knew his wife only too well. Had she answered him, she would certainly have said some utterly foolish thing which would have added to his misery, not reduced it in any way.

Ever since last evening, no one in the house was speaking to another. And, if compelled to do so, they spoke in whispers as though speaking aloud would be offensive or contrary to an unwritten code of conduct. Certainly, none would have spoken as loudly as Ghanshyamdas had done. Everyone was silent, withdrawn, lost in their own thoughts. Who was the most miserable, no one knew and so none tried to console the other.

How could Ghanshyamdas have spoken so loudly? Perhaps, it was his annoyance with his wife. She had started the packing early this morning but she was still not ready. They had as good as missed the two o'clock bus. Whether they'd even be able to make the next one wasn't at all sure. In all probability, they'd get late. He just couldn't imagine what state their daughter would be in over there - to bear this trauma at her age and alone with her three little children! And here was the girl's mother! She'd place one garment in the suitcase and then put her head in her hands and begun to cry. How would she ever get ready like this.

His anger had grown far greater than his grief. Almost as though his sorrow had been folded and pushed beneath his anger. May be that was why he'd been able to speak up so loudly...

But the instant he was annoyed, he regretted it. This anger was poison for him, real poison! The moment he lost his temper, all the blood in his body seemed to rush to his head. His face would get bloated and red, and like one drunk, he would say and do things without thinking. And how painful, truly painful was this tidal wave! When, like flood water, the anger ebbed, it left behind innumerable worms and snakes and insects and diseases. Ghanshyamdas would be left completely drained. His chest would ache, his breathing become laboured and painful, and every part of his body feel weak and listless.

And to think that only yesterday morning Ghanshyamdas had been dreaming of liberation. It was an innumerable family that he had raised. It didn't seem so much like his own offspring; rather more like a line outside a ration shop that would never come to an end. He would joke with his wife, "Parmeshwari! By the time you'll finish feeding the last child the first one will be hungry once again. That's how many children you have!'

Annoyed, Parmeshwari would grumble, "don't you eye my

children. Don't you worry. If I've given them birth, I'll feed them alright!"

To bring up so many children, educate them, find them jobs and then settle them in marriage, would have exhausted a much fitter man. And here was he; somehow, he'd lived out a long life with this sickly body of his. But he had worked patiently at his job and somehow responsibilities at home had got sorted out, one by one.

When he had finally retired last year he had sat down and done some stocktaking as it were, of his family. One must after all, take account of what had been accomplished and what still remained to be done, of how much energy he had now and how much time. This had reminded him of examination halls, and his own student days. Half an hour before a paper ended, when the warning bell rang, he would go through his answers and the question paper, rather like this. He'd check how many questions he had finished, how many had to be done, and how many remained. And only half an hour left! Having taken stock, he would settle down to write at just the right pace, so that he would finish them off in time. Otherwise, some tasks would surely be left undone. And to leave work incomplete, half-done, Ghanshyamdas didn't like that at all. One must fulfill one's responsibilities, no matter what value others set on them in the end.

It was somewhat in the same manner that he reviewed his life soon after his retirement.

His working-life was well and truly over. There was no chance of an extension and he knew he lacked the will to handle a new job. Was it not achievement enough that he had survived in this job with this worn out body of his! All the children had been put into adequate slots. What remained, were the two youngest and his duty towards them.

If only these two had listened like the others had! They too would have been settled before he retired. But each, in his way, had resisted his advice. Bittu had kept putting off marriage once she'd got a good job after her M. Sc. As for Raja, failing year after year, he had been unable to clear his B.A.

If only he had been able to fix up some employment for Raja and finished off with Bittu's marriage! How perfect things would have been! His pension would have sufficed for Parmeshwari and himself. They would have shifted to their village, to their own home. That way, they would save on the rent and escape the frightfully high costs of living in Delhi.

These two tasks…! He felt that the 'half- an-hour-left' bell was sounding its warning! If only he could somehow quickly manage to fulfill these two commitments within the next one year. His provident fund would cover the marriage expenses and he would somehow or the other, try to retain the official quarter.

Things had begun to fall into place. For the last few months, he had raced against time, just as he had done long ago, to face the challenge of the final half an hour in the exam hall. After that last effort, the bliss of freedom! The indescribable satisfaction of accomplishment! Yesterday morning, how longingly he had thought about this liberation from responsibility!

Only last week he had finalised a match for Bittu and got her engaged. As for the wedding - that was to be performed in three months. That left only Raja to worry about. What could he do with him…? Not one solution could he think of! Where was the guarantee that he *would* clear his exams this year, *and* get a decent job *and* become self-sufficient enough to fend for himself…

Ghanshyamdas felt that he was like an examinee who had completed the entire question paper, but just could not find the answer to a five-mark question. What should he do about these five marks? If Raja failed again, what was he to do with him? The wedding in three months' time would exhaust his provident fund and he would have to vacate his government quarter. Living in Delhi, would he be able to manage for the three of them, within his pension?

How much this unfinished five-mark question had troubled him, only he knew. Brooding about it day and night had often made him ill - that familiar stabbing pain cutting through his ribs would leave him writhing with pain on his *charpoy*.

And it was only yesterday morning he had contemplated his liberation. He had felt as though, in the panic of re-checking his paper, in the last five minutes of the examination, he had suddenly discovered that he had only to attempt five questions and that his paper was complete – that he was free to leave out one question, any one question! Leaving out the question of Raja's education was like that, wasn't it? Raja was himself to blame if he had failed to complete his studies. Ghanshyamdas had done everything that he could possibly have done. Now he would no longer consider Raja his responsibility. He had decided that he would omit that question. He would finish off Bittu's wedding, surrender the quarter and leave for his village before the year was over. Whatever Raja chose to do here in Delhi or elsewhere, that was for him to decide. It would be fine with Ghanshyamdas. If he came along with them, at least till he was alive, he'd be able to feed him in any case.

Now the paper was over! After the tussle of those three hours, how blessed was the peace that descended on him! He let everything slip away from him. How light he felt! The day's hard toil followed by the evening's well-deserved rest. A sense of fulfillment permeated his spirit.

Bittu's engagement had been a low-key affair. Where was the need for an ostentatious ceremony. It wasn't the first wedding in the family or anything. And, as everyone knew, he was now retired and if he weren't prudent, the provident fund money would run out long before the year was over

Simple though it was, all the children, except Indu, came to attend the engagement. Indu had written to congratulate them and had explained that she wouldn't be able to come to Delhi as Jagdish, her husband, was sick. She had written a long detailed letter saying how much she had wanted to come and how sorry she was to miss meeting everyone. She knew Chandigarh wasn't far from Delhi, but it wasn't easy for her to get away from the household routine. So the engagement would be a good opportunity to make a quick trip. But how could she leave her husband and come?

Ghanshyamdas had replied, telling her to write to them in detail about Jagdish's health. She should keep them informed about his recovery, and begin her preparations to come home for Bittu's wedding. No excuses would do at that time!

Everyone had now left after the engagement ceremony. Ghanshyamdas lay quietly on his *charpoy*, smiling softly to himself and feeling utterly at peace. He had already relinquished his government job and he was convinced that now he was to retire soon from the seemingly unending round of family duties. Just another month or two to go. These next few months were like the time spent by a passenger, with confirmed ticket in hand, waiting on the platform for the train to arrive. With baggage all booked in the brake-van he sits looking at the station clock wondering when the train will arrive so that he might quietly go and board the train and take his allotted seat. Ghanshyamdas reminded himself that he had attended to everything, it was now only a matter of time.

Earlier, at least a couple of times every day, he would pull up Raja about something or the other. If it wasn't about his studies, then it would be about his behaviour. Now, he'd given up saying anything at all to him. If he *did* happen to encounter him at home, a strange playfulness would overtake him – "he's an optional question, this wretch!" - he'd tell himself, and begin to smile - "where's the use of bothering with him!"

This made him marvel at himself. How had he been able to so distance himself from Raja that his career, his future, his studies, his job – nothing concerning him, could distress him any more. Truly, this was a fully retired man's attitude.

And it was in this relaxed mood last evening, as he lay on his *charpoy,* dozing off and enjoying the pleasures of retirement, that he had received the news of Jagdish – Indu's husband's - death…!

He read the telegram and just sat there silently, as if nothing had happened. Then, after a few moments, he wiped his glasses with the edge of his *dhoti* and read the telegram again. When he had read it once again, he called out to Parmeshwari. It was only when he heard his own voice that he had realised that he was crying; the tears rolling from his eyes turning his gaping mouth salty and his voice had become not only husky, it had also cracked.

Parmeshwari came running and so did Bittu. Even Raja seemed to have sensed – perhaps from the strange sound of his voice – that something was wrong. The three crowded around him and he sat there, telegram in hand, weeping.

Bittu took the telegram from his outstretched hand, read it and whispered quietly,

"Ma! Jagdish *jijaji* is no more…"

Parmeshwari uttered a piercing howl and something snapped inside Ghanshyamdas. He shouted, "go, go from here. Don't you pester me!"

The sound of wailing echoed from their house, sometimes from one of them and then from the other. But, in the end, all fell silent! The three of them sat in separate corners of the house and wept, while Raja stood on the terrace smoking and staring into the distance.

Extricating himself from the initial tide of grief, Ghanshyamdas felt a mild pain on the left side of his chest, but it wasn't severe enough to deserve his attention.

His thoughts were with Indu. How old was she – next June she would be thirty-five. This was hardly the age and with three little children, the youngest boy barely a year and a half. As for her in-laws – just one younger sister whom Indu had got married off only a year or two ago; parents-in-law, brothers-in-law – no one at all. Where could she go for help?

Most probably Jagdish had no insurance either – or maybe he had. He really didn't know. How much provident fund would he have? Any savings? No matter what he had, how long could it last?

To be widowed at her age, the trauma of loss, the dread of loneliness, all this was Indu's portion now; but what of the practical financial problems? Life lay endlessly before her - long, and full of struggle. The children to nurture, educate and settle. How was poor Indu going to cope? Who would support her now?

He checked himself. Maybe things weren't so hopeless after all. Accepted, there was none among Jagdish's family but here she had her own brothers and their wives, and her sisters... But he knew at once that there was no basis for these thoughts. If any of them had been ready to take responsibility for the family, would he have had to push himself at this age to manage Bittu's marriage? Those who were unwilling to look after younger brothers and sisters for only a year or two, could he expect them to shoulder the life-long responsibility of a widowed sister and her three small children? No... this was not a possibility.

Who then?

Nobody else. It could only be him. It would have to be him. Indu was his daughter. If he didn't support her at a time like this, who else would? Retired he certainly was but he wasn't dead. Then why should he wonder – who else?

Tomorrow morning they must catch the earliest bus for Chandigarh. Once the funeral was over, he would bring Indu and the children back here, home to Delhi.

Delhi – that reminded him – he was retired now, he would have to vacate this house. His pension was modest, and the provident fund money – that was for Bittu's marriage. Wasn't that important too? Surely he couldn't shut his eyes to that responsibility, could he? That money, he couldn't put aside for Indu. Besides, how long would it last, even if he did?

The state of his mind was like that of a candidate as he fills up the form for his examinations. He pauses time and again to ask himself if he is really prepared for the exam, will he be successful? But, more often than not, there is no opportunity to raise such questions. One has to take the exam even if one is not fully ready. Then the student has no choice but to convince himself that he is, in fact, ready…

The sum total was that he would have to set up a household once again, along with Parmeshwari, Indu and her three children. Once earlier, many years ago, he had set up home for the first time, but then only Parmeshwari had been with him and he had been young. Life had stretched before him, promising and bright. Now, standing on this other shore of life, he would have to start once again, make a fresh beginning! What *would* he do? With this unwilling sick body of his, what *would* he do? How would he earn? How would he make ends meet?

Going back to the village would be pointless. Finding a decent job there was impossible. And, even if he could buy some land, would he really be able to take to farming?

Then?

They would just have to continue in Delhi. But what would he achieve by staying here? Would he sell Coca-Cola or perhaps set up a *paan* and cigarette shop or…

He felt once again that he was back in the examination hall. As though, just as he was leaving the hall after finishing a three-hour paper, someone had handed him a new question paper and sent him back into the hall all over again. His legs ached, his back was stiff and his fingers numb with writing… and that new question paper, a full three-hour one. How can he start again?

But, what else was there to be done?

He pulled himself up, all of a sudden. Why was he anxious only about himself? What about Indu? Wasn't *she* the one who was most deeply affected by this disaster; the one who would have to pay the heaviest price?

After thirty five years of living her life in a certain way, she too would have to begin all over again. There would be no companion by her side. She could no longer rightfully demand, her children could never throw a tantrum, to have their wishes fulfilled. They would be guests in this house, dependent on his charity – dependent on one who might depart this world at any moment. No one could tell when something might trigger that knife-like pain in his ribs – send it slinking up his body to cut off and put an end to everything…

Ghanshyamdas' blood ran cold. He was terrified. He was mortally afraid of that pain, sharp like a knife, and he knew then that he did not have the courage to thump his chest and say, "Indu, my girl! As long as I am around, what have you to fear?"

How could he make such a promise? His entire life had been passed seated behind a desk in a musty government office and now, in his old age, he would sell cold drinks, peddle packs of cigarettes! He was in a sorry shape – breathless and fatigued if he sat up even for half an hour! And *he* would sit minding a shop?

He wondered – was it not possible for Indu herself to make a new beginning? After all, she was younger than he was. It would be easier for her to adjust to a new life. She had in any case to struggle, then why shouldn't she be the one to start afresh?

But how?

Dim images began to pass before him. And, one by one, he swept them aside. No! He could never ask his daughter to do any of these things. Wasn't it possible for Indu to be married once again? Married…? Bittu was younger, prettier and better educated, and doing a good job – how difficult it had been for him to fix up a match for her – then, what was the chance for Indu with her three children?

No – he set his head purposefully – nothing of the kind. *I* must be the one to make a fresh start. A father and to think like this was a shame.

"Parmeshwari! Are you ready?" He stood up.

His stick held firmly in his hand, his brows furrowed into resolute lines, he stood up and looked around sternly. Yes, he had the ability to start again. What has age to do with it. It was all a matter of courage and there was no shortage of that.

Unsought, there surfaced from underneath the firm set lines of his face, the mischievous laughter of a precocious child: "perhaps you can deceive others, maybe even Indu, but how are you going to fool yourself, Ghanshyamdas?"

His hand slackened on the cane. It had begun to tremble in his hand.

"How wonderful it would be, if Indu mustered up the courage," he thought to himself, "but how could he tell her this?"

He coughed loudly. And that stabbing pain had begun to rattle the ribs on his left.

IN THE LAND OF LIGHT

Lying there on the hospital bed, his old, infirm body felt completely worn out. He had discovered these past few weeks, that you could actually feel exhausted just lying on a bed. Every limb ached. In all his sixty years, he had never spent this much time in a hospital. Today it was exactly nine weeks.

The first week in hospital he had spent lying around, sitting about on the bed, simply waiting for his turn. In those days there was nothing for him to do. Sitting around vacantly, he had got bored, like he was today. When he'd feel fatigued, he'd chat sometimes with bed number thirty seven or else thirty nine. But this talk did not refresh him. In this ward each spoke only of his problems or of his family. Not a single happy thing did they talk about. The atmosphere made him feel worse. Bored stiff he would get up and stroll around. But how risky that was. He could not make out the odd, everyday things placed on the floor. Sometimes a glass would roll over, at others a bedpan would clang or else he would bump onto a stool.

The trouble was that from a distance, he couldn't even make out if someone was approaching. By the time he would find out he would be too close. No matter how hard he tried, occasionally he would end up colliding.

Lying there he had started playing different games. He knew there was this clock on the wall at the far end of the ward. The nurses and attendants used it to tell the time. He had heard it's bell that chimed every half hour. Sometimes, when the ward was deathly silent, as it often is on summer afternoons, he could even hear the clock's own sound - tik-tik. He'd imagine the pendulum swinging to that sound – dhak-dhak!

He'd grown quite fond of that pendulum somehow – the way one often gets attached with one thing or the other when one is sick. He would think of the pendulum as a dear confidante of his. After all, everything hinges on that pendulum. It swings and so time passes. And time passes so that his turn might come. It's to make his turn come swiftly that the pendulum works day and night, day and night......

When the clock game bored him, he would try to make out the different sounds in the ward. The fellow with the persistent cough must be right at the back to the left somewhere. And that constant groaning, that comes from the right. Ghurr-ghurr, thak-thak..... that's the trolley, the one they make the patients lie down on, to take them about. Click-click.... that sharp sound was of the nurses' sandals. And the sense of walking without a sound was of the doctor's crepe soles.

When a week later he had his operation, things had again changed. A full two months now he had been lying in this altered condition. His eyes had been bandaged. He couldn't see a thing. Earlier, he could make out things that were nearby. Dimly perhaps, but something at least. Whether the person standing close by was an attendant or a doctor, that much he could at least find out. Now, he could make out nothing. Not even the difference between night and day.

How tedious these two months had been!

The bandage had been on for so long that it seemed as if he had never seen anything with his own eyes. Brooding endlessly, this idea had now lodged itself so deeply in his mind that he'd begun to actually believe it.

Before the operation, when everything was blurred and dim, how determined he'd been to see the world the way other people did. How terrible he felt when a group photo was brought home and he couldn't recognise his sons in that sea of faces because the photos had been so small. What a sorry figure he cut when he'd address one son mistaking him for the other. Or say something to his daughter thinking her to be his daughter-in-law, or the other way around!

God knows when a sense of inferiority had begun to seep into him. Because of his faint vision, he could never dare to think of himself as equal to others. How could he, when he himself had never accepted the idea.

When his elder son, Girish had spoken of the operation, he'd laughed it off. "When it's been this way all my life, my son what can be done now? And now what's the use?"

After all, what was the use of an operation? He'd been taking one treatment or the other his entire life. When nothing had helped, then what would change now? As it was, his condition had become much worse. Every day, things were deteriorating. Besides this wasn't any old treatment, it was an operation, after all.

All the other things could be managed, but what about the money? Where was that to come from? Now, when he was earning nothing – couldn't earn anything actually – would it be proper to put such a heavy burden on his sons? These poor fellows earning just about enough to manage!

How much Girish had urged and begged him. Finally, when he had sworn that he would get it done, then the father could no longer resist.

Bowing before Girish's stubbornness, he'd landed himself here.

After the surgery, when he regained consciousness, how irksome the bandage had been. A deep fear had slowly crept into his mind. He had tried valiantly to stamp out that fear. But the little hatchling had grown into a fully grown snake and now into a king cobra, it hissed and terrorised his mind. He couldn't see clearly. Granted, he couldn't see distant things. He had a problem reading. Excessive heat and cold made his eyes swell. But then, he wasn't completely blind.

But, persuaded by Girish, he had gone and got this thing done! His eyes were bandaged and he was counting every passing day. The doctor, of course, said the operation had gone off well. Once the bandage is removed, his eyes would be fine. He'd see the world perfectly, with healthy eyes, the way other people did.

But till the bandage was taken off, one couldn't say anything for sure. It was quite possible that some error might have occurred. But this one would know only when the bandage comes off and then he would no longer be able to see even the blurred picture of the world that he had got so used to.

This fear had possessed him from the start. This worry clouded his days and robbed his nights of sleep. Tossing in his bed he had cursed the moment of weakness when he'd succumbed to Girish's emotional blackmail and agreed to the operation. Gradually his doubts melted away and then evaporated altogether. Everyday someone or the other in the ward had the operation and they all got well. Very rarely did any operation fail. Why then would the doctors bungle his case! After all, they weren't his enemies.

This slender ray of hope brightened by the day and good cheer suffused his mind. More than the doctors, it was Girish who reassured him the most. After the operation he had stayed in the hospital with him for a week.

For these past two months, he had viewed the future with a child-like faith. Today, at 10 o'clock, the bandage was to be removed. Girish was also to arrive by the 12 o'clock train. How many things were to happen in this one day!

And just then the clock in the ward struck eight. Only two hours more for the bandages to come off!

How much he'd mused about his future in these last two weeks! So much so that he had somehow convinced himself that the operation had been a complete success and he was going to get back his sight – which, in a sense, he'd never really had before.

And, all at once, somewhere deep within him a clock seemed to ring out sharp and clear. How could he be so sure. Yes, operations are almost always successful, but some did go wrong. How could he take for granted that his operation wasn't one of those? Suppose his was actually a failure? All these little fledglings of hope that he'd nurtured, what would become of them? These tiny chicks of hope were the creation of his mind. Now, they'd opened their little eyes. How clear the perfectly round yellow rings in their eyes were. Would he be able to bear the cruel loss of so many innocent little chicks in a single stroke?

A wave of anger swept over him….. it drenched his entire being. That anger spared no one- not Girish, nor the doctors. What a precipitous edge they'd brought and stood him on – that's what he was brooding about. He himself had never nourished the dream of seeing the world clearly. He didn't even remember if his eyes had ever been normal. Where then was the need for him to be shown such enticing visions in his old age? And now, when he'd put his faith in these dreams, if they failed, then what? Would his brittle, aged mind be able to bear this shock… The trauma of such a deep disappointment could stop the beating of his heart - he took a deep breath to calm himself. The heart beat? What could one say of that? The intense joy of sight restored could as well stop it too. And he felt that someone had taken down that clock on the far wall of the ward and fitted it right inside him. And the pendulum, it was swinging resolutely inside, striking the walls of his skull - thok! thok! thok!

He mopped the sweat from his forehead and turned over his

side. He was not going to think about the future, not about the untying of the bandage either. Nor worry about whether he was getting back his sight or not. Sixty years were over. Who knew how much longer he had to live. In any case getting or not getting his sight was no big deal for him.

As for his vision, it had been rotten like this for God knows how long. It wasn't a question of how long. As far as he could remember that's how long it had always been. How clearly he remembered that day even now. He was in the fourth standard when he had not been able to do the sum because he couldn't read the numbers on the board. How mercilessly his teacher had beaten him. He'd gone on protesting that he couldn't see the figures, couldn't read them on the board. And *Masterji* had continued to flog him "yes! sure you can't read the figures! You'd have to solve the sum then, wouldn't you, you wretch! Want to play the fool with me, do you? Don't you worry, I'll make you see the figures just now!"

Sobbing and whimpering and rubbing his back, he'd made his way home along with the news of his inability to read the numbers on the board. How furious his father had been. Why hadn't they told him about it before? *Babuji* was angry with everyone. How he'd scolded *Masterji* – how dare he beat his delicate child? He'd be foolish to think he could survive in his job if he annoyed the senior clerk in the British Company's Office.

He was mad with his wife too. He knew the poor child had inherited these defective eyes from her. But where was the sense in pulling her up for this?

From then on had begun the perpetual shuttling from one doctor to another. All kinds of medicines had been used but nothing had worked. Very often, there would be this swelling in his eyes which would damage his retina. The swelling persisted and there was no other treatment left for them to try. The doctors felt helpless too.

And then *babuji* had been transferred. They'd gone to the Kullu hills. That particular day was sharply etched in his memory. *Babuji* was away on tour and *Amma's* friend, Zubeida *chachi* had dropped by. Home remedies, little charms and magical cures, she knew them all. She was the saviour of the entire town. *Amma* brought up the problem of her little darling's eyes. Zubeida *chachi* lifted his eye-lids and peered into his eyes. Wringing her hands she exclaimed - "*hai behenji*! Why on earth are you troubling the little fellow! Call this a problem! I'll set it right just now........" and she had bustled off briskly. When she returned *chachi* brought a root with her. He didn't now remember the name of the tree. How pungent, how strong that root had been – as sharp as a blade, stinging and burning his eyes beyond bearing. *Chachi* claimed that she would scrape the eyes, and everything would be fine.

Amma was eager to quickly cure her child and wipe off the sin of having given birth to a defective offspring, and in a single stroke, please her husband too! And taking that root, Zubeida *chachi* had scraped at his eyes and bloodied them thoroughly. For ages afterwards, his eyes had been dressed and bandaged.

When *babuji* returned from his tour, he could have wept in frustration. There was utter pandemonium at home. He was completely fed up with his foolish wife. And *babuji* was the one who had been the most troubled of all. And it continued so even today.

His entire life had been handed over to doctors. Both his younger brothers had finished their studies and become officers and he, courtesy *babuji's* contacts, had worked at one petty job after the other. Not one decent job had he got his whole life. The doctors had said quite plainly that his eyes had been so severely damaged and scarred that nothing could be done.

Ultimately, accepting this as his fate, he'd made his compromise with life. Not once these sixty years had the possibility been considered that he could see clearly.

Time had gone by. He wasn't the guardian of his children anymore. Quite the opposite, in fact. He'd stopped worrying about himself. Then, one day, Girish had brought home a friend of his, "This is my friend, Dr. Kashyap. He's recently returned from the UK after specialising in eye treatment."

"Wonderful!" he had laughed, a mirthless little laugh, "it's a pleasure to meet you, doctor *sahib*! But you've come far too late. I've abandoned all hope by now."

He knew why Girish had brought Dr. Kashyap home. Girish too sensed what was passing through his mind. He knew that the eye-problem was his sore point. Speaking about it didn't help at all. Rather, it was like probing an old wound. Only a reminder that he couldn't see clearly at all.

"*Pitaji*! Forgive me! You……" Girish probably wanted to explain. Dr. Kashyap stopped him mid way, "It doesn't matter, Verma *sahib*! It's natural for patients to get disheartened – but what's a doctor worth if he also abandons hope? It's cases like these which are the real test….." and Dr. Kashyap's tone had turned very gentle, "If I examine your eyes, you wouldn't have any objection, would you?"

Why hadn't he been able to say 'no'. A little hope must have lurked somewhere in his aged soul – could this be the doctor destined for glory!

Dr. Kashyap had a good look at his eyes. He took his time and then left asking him to come to his clinic the following day.

After examining him for half an hour, he looked up and smiled, "no harm done yet, Girish! I tell you, take *pitaji* to the Medical Institute in Delhi."

"But what will they do? " He hadn't liked the doctor talking to Girish. Why doesn't the doctor explain things to him. He understood his own problem best, knew all about the umpteen treatments he'd had – what on earth did Girish know!

"Look!" the doctor explained, "The scars on the membrane covering your eyes have blurred your vision. Suppose we operate and actually replace this membrane......"

"Can this really be done, doctor!" His words expressed the accumulated hopelessness of years.

"This is a commonplace procedure nowadays!" The doctor had smiled.

For how many days on end had, there been this tug of war over expenses. When he had failed to fulfill his duty as a father, by what right could he put this unnecessary burden on his sons? But Girish had simply refused to listen and here he was.

Just then the ward clock struck nine thirty.

"Only half an hour more!" he mused.

He didn't know why, but he was convinced that the operation wasn't a success. The doctor would remove the bandage and ask him. He'd blink his eyes and would still not see anything. He'd laugh and say – "doctor, please remove the bandage first!" And with a strange look the doctor would say, "oh! It is unsuccessful!" And he would chortle loudly and say – "I had told you so but who listens to me?

Thak-thak! clatter-clatter! The sound distracted him. Someone had brought the trolley into the ward. They would load someone on to it and take him away. Someone to be operated? Or may be, a bandage to be removed...click-click the sound of a nurse's heels.

He felt the trolley had stopped next to his bed. Perhaps it was him they had come to fetch. Nine thirty had struck quite some time ago. It must be about to be ten. His bandage was to be removed at ten.

The nurse's steps stopped at his bedside. Then he heard the shuffling of papers. They must be scanning his case history hanging up on the wall. So many of them had looked at his records. If someone took a look and then just walked away he wouldn't have a clue who it was – doctor, nurse, compounder, sweeper or someone else.

"Get up please! Bed number thirty-eight!" said the record reader, "your bandage is to be removed". It was the familiar voice of the morning nurse.

"Bhaiya, get up!" Whose could this male voice be? He sat up. Actually, it was a familiar voice. This same person had put him umpteen times on a trolley to take him to the doctor for his checkup. Was he a compounder, a peon or a sweeper, he had often wondered. Yes! Let the bandage come off, he'd see for himself. He laughed somewhere deep within. How easily he had assumed that his eyes would be fine!

That same person slipped one arm around his shoulders and the other beneath his knees and slid him onto the trolley. On the first day, when this same fellow had dragged him this way, how furious he had been – "come on! what the hell! I'm not a bedroll or a trunk!" But they probably dragged everyone this way. They did this from morning to evening! How careful could they be with each and every case! He no longer felt annoyed with this fellow any more.

The trolley moved off – ghrr-ghrr! thak-thak! And alongside, the click-click of heels! From the pace of the trolley, he guessed they had reached the end of the ward. And when the trolley jerked he knew they had left the ward. The trolley stopped for a moment. A short conversation at the duty room – bed number thirty eight to go to Dr. Sharma for removal of bandage. And the trolley set off again ghrr-ghrr !

Turning left, down the slope they went. Now they were headed for the doctor's room. The trolley stopped again. Maybe they had reached.

They helped him up and seated him on a chair. The room

was rather cold and the chair had a thick cushion. He realised they had seated him on a chair in the doctor's room not on the bench outside. He sat patiently. There was not a sound that he could hear.

All of a sudden, he sensed someone around. The rustle of clothes and with it, the thok-thok of shoes.

"And how are you, Verma *sahib*?" It was Dr. Sharma's voice.

"Well, thank you doctor!" he replied unenthusiastically.

"Then, shall we remove your bandage?" Dr. Sharma's tone was light, casual.

"As you please."

Damn! That talk of bandages again, just what he would rather forget about now. Dr. Sharma was unfailingly pleasant. Then why was he so cold, so indifferent, so lifeless? The doctor could also feel hurt, couldn't he?

"How do you feel, Mr. Verma?" He could feel the doctor's touch on his head, "excited?"

"Yes, a bit doctor!" he said softly.

And the pressure of the bandage on his head began to ease. Steadily the bandage began to slip. He felt he was turning numb. There was no sensation in him at all. There were a hundred things he should have felt at this time. But what was he experiencing? Nothing at all. He was without feeling of any kind. What had happened to him? He felt drained of all excitement. Had excess of excitement rendered him incapable of sensation?

The last inner edge of the bandage and the cotton wool pad fell into his lap. The bandage was off – Now? Now?

"How are you?" the doctor asked

"… …" he said nothing.

"Don't get excited." The doctor gently stroked his eyes, "open your eyes slowly."

He sat lifeless, immobile. Then, using all the energy at his command he raised his eyelids, his eyes opened – and then, nothing. All dark – just as it was with the bandage on. He blinked his eyes a couple of times and the curtains of darkness began to lift – haze – smoke -dispersing smoke - and everything was clear!

He stood up.

"Be seated," the doctor urged him, pressing him down onto his chair with his hands on his shoulders – "can you see?"

"Everything, doctor!" He looked up and saw the doctor, a child-like delight in his eyes. Then he looked at the nurse standing nearby. Saw the chair. His own hands resting on the arms of the chair....

"Good! Congratulations."

"Thank you so much, doctor! Thank you very much."

Switching on the torch in his hand, the doctor examined his eyes thoroughly for quite some time. "Everything is alright," he said, "I'm giving you a medicine. Put a few drops in the eyes for a month. Everything is fine."

"May I go home, doctor?" He felt that he could not stay here another moment. He wanted to meet his wife and children. Wanted to tell them he could now see everything...

"It will take me an hour or two to get your papers ready, then you can go," the doctor said, "sister, take the patient back to his bed."

"I will go back myself" And he walked out of the room. How clear everything looked – the verandah, the room, the furniture! How sharply he saw everything. He could make it on his own. No longer was he afraid of stumbling on the stairs. Without any hesitation, he could jump across any drain.

He entered his ward. On the left, he saw that perpetual "cougher". On the right, the one whimpering with pain; he could see him too.

He sat down on his bed.

Turning around, he looked at the wall clock. This was the tick-tock he had been hearing all along. This was the pendulum he had been visualising. But now he could actually see the clock and watch the pendulum swinging. At any instant, he could tell if it was on the right or on the left. And from this far he could read the figures on the clock. From this far....right here sitting on his bed. And that day how viciously *masterji* had beaten him because he had been unable to read the figures on the board. Let them give him a sum now...he'd sit right at the back of the class and read off every figure.....

...And then, something happened to him.

..."Now I can see - when I am sixty years old. Now, when I cannot go back to school. Cannot take up a job. When my children have proceeded so far in their lives that I can neither teach them nor guide them. Now, when willy-nilly they have shaped their lives as best they could." Even if he had not got back his sight, how could it have mattered? It was not as if he would be beaten for not solving a sum anymore!

Had he got back his sight earlier, then his sons, like their cousins, would have been officers too. Would not have felt inferior before their relations, not become passive door-mats. What would he do with this vision now?

Sitting on his bed, he was waiting for Girish who would come by the 12 o'clock train. How glad he'd be to see him. He would say, "I told you, you'd become absolutely fit. You need not have resisted."

There was no denying Girish had given him his sight. He had every right to claim so. But he must admit, he felt not a trace of gratitude towards Girish. He overflowed only with a deep anger for his son. No tenderness at all. How perfect his life was till now. He had accepted his handicap as his destiny. If there was deprivation in his life, or that of his children, how could he be blamed? He was himself helpless. What had Girish given him…sight? Yes, he could now see sharp and clear. Yes, he could see…..he had got this one life, a life which had gone seriously wrong because of his handicap. He wanted to right that wrong now that he'd virtually finished his life's journey. But he could not do that. How could he do that! He could not re-live the past, could he? How would he bear the bitterness of a wasted, worthless life? How could he feel grateful to Girish! How could Girish ever know what Girish had given him.

KAPOOR

Black drainpipe pants, shoes pointed as a nib, a dazzling white shirt straight out of an ad., Castro-like flowing beard, huge tapering moustache and crew-cut hair. That was Kapoor.

I can't say what was the reason, but from the day he arrived, everyone in the hostel knew who Kapoor was. At that time, I still didn't know him. But, when I think of it now, I am sure that Kapoor did have an unmistakable aura, because somehow, he just could not be any different.

Early next morning, there was this paper stuck on the hostel notice board. The good old warden's first sermon telling us that this was a hostel, not our home. That a hostel was somewhere midway between home and a hotel and that he would be obliged if we treated it as such.

But I think a hostel is more a cross between a home and a hospital. Don't you think so?

And everyone I met, made it a point to tell me that this was Kapoor's doing. Unquestioningly, I too accepted that he was the one behind it. In any case, I did know for sure, that I hadn't done it.

I must admit that I didn't like it at all. In a single day, Kapoor was cock of the roost. My pride was hurt. I found it humiliating to accept that a fresher should put all the senior boys in the shade. That must have been the reason why I gave no importance either to that slip on the notice board, or to Kapoor himself.

But the very next day, he came along and accosted me. "Excuse me," he said, "I've heard, Mr. Kohli sir, that you are from Bihar?"

"Yes, you've heard right, sir!" I said.

"The fact is..." he spoke most courteously, "that I've also come from Bihar."

"So?" I raised my eyebrows.

"What if I desire your friendship..."

And suddenly the old devil in me was aroused. Such a senior student and he just a fresher! Thinks he's the cat's whiskers!

"On one condition." My mouth was set grimly.

"Yes?"

"Let's not see you with this beard." Without waiting for his answer I nudged him aside and walked away.

He had irritated the hell out of me, demanding my friendship in this way. It was an unmannerly intrusion upon my self-esteem and injured my vanity. I felt like a beaten dog left to whine and whimper. At that moment, I could have barked at anyone, or bitten someone.

Next morning, a loud knocking on the door woke me up. I had been reading till pretty late into the night and, as it was Sunday, the plan was to sleep till ten or eleven. It was about 9.30. Involuntarily, my hand picked up the cane lying under my bed. I felt like thrashing whoever was at the door. Grabbing the towel from the chair I wrapped it around myself and opened the door.

"I'm Kapoor," the boy standing there said.

The relevance of his self-introduction struck even my half-awake senses. He had abandoned not only his beard but also his whiskers in Cuba, and stood clean-shaven before me, smooth as a billiard ball.

The cane fell from my hand and my face broke into a grin, "how come Kapoor, first thing today…?"

"You asked me to," he submitted. "You didn't want to see me with that beard. So early today I had it shaved off and came to your room, but you were asleep. I had been waiting for you in the dining hall but you didn't show up. So here I am."

"Come in, come, sit!" I moved out of the way.

Something melted within me. All my anger at him vanished. For a long time we sat and chatted the way I do with my younger brother, or perhaps I might with a beloved.

He told me a great many things about himself. He came from a really affluent family. They had a house in Delhi that was rented out. But they had kept a portion for their own use. They had a car here too. Anyone from home who visits, uses it. He had stayed in many hostels early on in life. Now he was in a hostel again! He had wanted his mother to come to Delhi. They would keep a servant and stay in their own home. But he didn't know why his father had not agreed. So here he was, back in a hostel. He was very lonely and depressed too.

Sometimes he seemed like a child, utterly vulnerable, at others, mature and experienced. It was difficult to say which was his real self or was he in reality, an extraordinary mix of the two.

I met Kapoor on his way out of the dining hall when I went for lunch. He wasn't alone. There was a bunch of boys with him, all of them talking loudly. Kapoor was clearly their leader. This wasn't the solitary pensive Kapoor of the morning, but one in positively high spirits. He greeted me with an exceedingly sweet, 'hello'.

"And how's life Mr.Kapoor sir?" I asked in regular hostel style.

"Major problem, sir," desperation written all over his face.

"Why, what's up?" I asked sobering up.

"Had to get up while eating," he said.

"Oh!" I laughed, things weren't as serious as he made out.

"Why, you have a class straight after lunch?"

"No sir!" he answered softly, "my stomach gets full!"

And chortling loudly, he marched on with his friends.

After that I never saw Kapoor downcast.

When I visited his room, I was in for a big surprise. There were huge posters on three of the walls – of Indian and foreign actresses. Nude, and semi-nude. On the fourth was a grand picture of Hanumanji.

"What's this, Kapoor?" I asked, "what's this confirmed ascetic doing in your harem?"

"Kohli sahib, the fact is...," he gravely explained, "our scriptures tell us that what's worth doing is worth doing well. When I sit at my desk to study, all I see before me is Hanumanji. A student you'll agree should be a complete *brahmachari*, and what greater inspiration than Hanumanji, the ultimate yogi. Whose picture should I put here then?"

"Okay...okay...but then, why the film stars...?"

"I don't study all the time," he said. "When I'm free or about to sleep, then I lie down, like this," and he lay with his head towards Hanumanjij's picture. The three walls that he could now view clearly were those with the pictures of the starlets.

"Wonderful arrangement, Kapoor!" I admired.

"But last night there was a major tragedy!" he said in a mournful tone. I looked at him silently.

He got off the bed and went to the cupboard.

"At night this cupboard door got opened up like this," and he opened the door to demonstrate. On the inside there was a picture, a foot and a half long, of a nude woman.

"I woke up suddenly at night, and felt that something was wrong." He elaborated, narrating the events of the night. "I put on the light, and what should I see but this dame with downcast modest eyes gazing at the opposite wall. I spun around and there was Hanumanji wreathed in smiles, ogling her and she glancing back coyly at him…"

"Quiet, you shameless fellow!" my latent religious loyalties making me jump to the deity's defence. "You won't spare even the gods and goddesses!"

"Hey! What's the big deal!" He sounded outraged, "tell the truth and you thing I'm joking. From tonight I'll lock the cupboard before sleeping. I'm convinced Hanumanji rather enjoys the scene…"

I got up and left. I was still thinking of his gallery of pictures when, passing that way next, I saw that the walls of his room were bare. Not a picture in sight. When I asked, he explained somberly that a couple of days ago his brother and sister-in-law had dropped by. He had asked a friend to keep his dinner for him and so left the room keys with him. The stupid fellow had opened the room and seated them there. Well, they saw the exhibition of pictures and left word for him to come and meet them urgently. When he got back, he had pulled down and thrown away all the pictures. Now he was busy avoiding his brother, and hadn't been to see him yet.

"But Kapoor, you room looks quite forlorn," I laughed. "No colour, no…"

"Yes Kohli sahib, I feel the same too," he said, humbly accepting my verdict. "I'm doing the best I can…" and he threw open the cupboard door. Gone was the nude woman, and in her place were stuck brightly coloured posters of birds and butterflies.

He moved near the bed. Bending down he tugged the string tied to the leg of his bed. Out came a pigeon. "Last night I caught this," he said, "when brother comes next, I'll present it to him."

And then, all at once, all sounds of laughter, all activities ceased. Four or five students from our hostel had gone to the Yamuna for a swim. The current was swift. One of them had drowned. All of us had been caught up in the search that day. We had run around from morning, but his body had not been found. Kapoor and I had been together. He had worked the hardest of all. Tired and defeated, when we had given up and sat down by the river, it was Kapoor who had run off to the bazaar and brought food for everyone.

We were worn out: physical exhaustion on the one hand, disappointment and sorrow on the other. When we returned, I had left early to go to bed.

The warden had sent for me first thing in the morning, "what was going on at night in your block, Mr.Kohli?"

"At night, sir?" I asked. "I'm afraid I don't know. I was tired and fast asleep."

"Last night," the warden said, "Kapoor from your block and his buddies, gave the boys a rough time. They told them that the drowned student had been seen in his room, studying at his table. There was plenty of shouting. Now, no one is ready to occupy the rooms next to his. Many of the boys refused to sleep alone and doubled up with each other."

"I'm sorry, I have no idea," I pleaded innocence.

"You didn't even hear the screaming?"

"No, sir!"

"That's strange," he said. "I could hear them even out here. How soundly do you sleep? Besides, there have been complaints earlier that they stay up all night and disturb others till one or one thirty."

"Sorry, sir, I'll keep an eye on things." I came away.

The story of the drowned student's ghost had caught on quite strongly. Many of the freshers moved in with relatives and were not willing to return. There were complaints about the noise at night. Kapoor and his gang were given a thorough dressing down and he had been fined ten rupees.

But the fine was of no use. The noise at night didn't stop, it only got worse. Even I woke up despite my deep sleep.

In the dead of night, a loud voice rang out from one end of the hostel, "what's the news?"

In response from the other side, came the answer, "Chou is stewed!"

And after this brief prelude they would begin a regular series of slogans. It sounded almost as if a political meeting was on in the hostel. The volume kept on increasing, until the sounds must definitely have reached the warden's residence, in one corner of the hostel. I felt like getting up and scolding them, and once and for all, settle Kapoor as well. But we were at war with China at that time. What could I say to Kapoor who went around all day spreading his patriotic messages! What if the warden called me again in the morning? But no such summons came. Confronted with this unabated barrage of patriotism even the warden could do nothing.

Shortly afterwards it was vacation time. Everyone had packed up and was ready to go home, though this didn't affect me. The hostel was really peaceful during the holidays and that is when one could study undisturbed. I had made up my mind well in advance that I would stay back and finish off my thesis.

Kapoor came to me, "Kohli sahib, you're going home for the holidays?"

"No," I replied, "I'm planning to stay back and study."

"Okay, okay…" A look of pleasure shone on his face. Perhaps

he too wanted to stay back. How comfortable he was in the hostel! No worry of home. He was undoubtedly the most boisterous of us all…

Merely a formality, I asked, "you're going?"

"What will I do at home!" He got up, "what's the point in going home. I've always been in a hostel, I've grown up in hostels," he said heading for the door. His back towards me, "I must have even been born in a hostel. I think my parents were also born in a hostel…" and he left the room.

I saw Kapoor was seated on the veranda wall upstairs. His face was flushed red. He looked like a barbarian to me. Below, there was a row of taxis. Each student's baggage would be loaded, he would take leave of his friends, and get into the taxi as it would move off. As each taxi departed, Kapoor would shout the most vulgar obscenities from above. None was spared. I had never seen this facet of his personality. I climbed upstairs.

"What's the matter, Kapoor?"

"Why are they going home?" He wasn't quite in control of himself.

"Why don't you go too?" I asked.

"My father doesn't want me to…!" I felt that his eyes were brimming with tears, his voice had cracked. He turned the other way and left.

By night the hostel was virtually empty. The corridors were deserted. It was late in the night when, from a far off corner of the hostel, I heard a loud stamping of shoes and a tuneless voice singing out:

"When my heart is grief-stricken in *sawan*, I down a peg or two…"

It was Kapoor's voice. I didn't make a move to get up or leave my room. I just sat there.

"Hey you ! Guard !" Kapoor's voice rang out.

"Yes sir!" from way out somewhere he answered.

"You've brought the chess?"

"Yes Sir!"

"Come, we'll play…through the night…all night."

And the sounds from the common room began. Kapoor was laughing uproariously and spewing filthy abuse.

They didn't let me sleep all night. The infinite desperation hidden in his voice haunted me. In the morning, when the sounds died down, I went to the common room to have a look. Lying beside the guard, Kapoor lay sleeping in a drunken stupor.

THE WITHERED BRANCH

It was past seven o'clock and Baby still wasn't back. I felt very irritated. This soon turned to anger: why hadn't she come back as yet! Was it fair to stay out for hours together. I didn't like it one bit, she had left at four and was seven now. Appa doesn't pull her up that's why all the younger kids have got out of hand. Poor Amma, she is laid up in bed all the time. She hadn't been able to teach us children anything or guide us in any way. She simply gave birth and left it at that.

Appa doesn't scold us any longer, but he wasn't like that earlier. Anna, Bhaskar and I... Appa used to scold us a lot and Anna and Bhaskar were even beaten. Appa's temper, my god! It used to scare the hell out of us. An incarnation of Durvasa! Let him once be provoked, then no mercy for anyone. It must be the same temper that is stuffed to the brim in Anna and Bhaskar.

But Appa isn't the same anymore. I can't remember him ever scolding Ramu, Baby or Radha! Those three, they are Appa's darlings! I don't know, maybe as one ages, one softens up. He just isn't as strict anymore. It really amazes me the things these children are up to these days. The three of us older ones used to fall silent if we as much as saw Appa. And these three – Baby goes on singing film songs all day and gets away with it.

It isn't as if Appa does not get angry any longer, it's just that he doesn't show it. The day he is angry, he'll simply not eat.

I think I too have inherited this temper from him. It was this same temper that made me think of Baby again and again. So I flew off the handle when she returned. "Where have you been all this time?"

"Akka, I had gone to Bholi's house to play."

"Is this the time to play?" I twisted her ear.

"No, it's the time to pull my ears Akka!" Baby was smiling. Her eyes brimmed with fearlessness born of trust.

I was furious, "the wretch is joking," and leaving her ear, I gave her a tight slap.

Her smile vanished and a smoldering sort of anger surfaced on her face. But she didn't weep as I feared she might.

At that very moment Ramu surfaced singing his own tune.

"When Akka slaps Baby what can I do? I can run off!"

And before I could get hold of him and give him one too, he ran off.

By now my anger had cooled but the irritation lingered in a most virulent form, irritation not at Baby or Ramu but at myself.

How does it matter if she does come a little late, it isn't such a big thing – all children go to play. Didn't I play too. Where was the need to beat her? It was as if I had ripped off a smiling mask from a doll's face and put an angry one in its place.

But why shouldn't I be upset. When it's late and the children haven't come home, I get worried. Children should finish their dinner by seven. If they keep roaming around till nine, they'll eat only at ten and when will I get free and when do I study?

But it isn't only the children. If Anna, Bhaskar or Appa get late and don't finish their dinner on time I feel very unsettled. I feel completely helpless. Of course I don't spare them when they are late. Even Appa has to face my scolding. If it gets really late and he doesn't have a decent excuse, then like Baby, Ramu or

Radha, he tip-toes into the house and sits quietly somewhere. And he looks to me just like a little child! But do they ever get upset at my chiding – never! As for Anna I simply refuse to serve him and he follows me around begging, "Shyamali, forgive me just this once. I won't be late from tomorrow."

"No! No! Anna, you make it as late as you like everyday!" I tell him gently, "how does it matter to me. Only no one gets any dinner, that's all. Just as well, I needn't cook in the evening, just sit and study."

But he wouldn't be silenced. He would plead again and again: "Shyamali, my good, my dear Akka! If I'm late again you just make me stand in the corner."

And then Radha would materialise from nowhere and entreat on his behalf, "come on Akka, give him food, poor Anna he's famished."

Anna would then set about flattering Radha, as if I would give him his dinner only on her recommendation. But the poor fellow must be hungry, and then, he is my elder brother, a strapping huge six foot three fellow sitting there so obediently before me! I serve him his rice, *rasam* and *sambhar* and lecture him alongside, "listen Anna, don't come late from now."

How many times has our Mausi told me, "the way you carry on Shyamali one would think Anna is still a little baby."

Poor Mausi, I tell myself, she can't understand. Perhaps she has never known what affection means. A widow poor thing and no children either. If she had wanted she could have treated us as her children, she is our aunt after all. Couldn't she have been a mother to her forever-ill sister's children? But she couldn't do that and she has reaped the fruits of that too. She lives with us all right but no one talks to her much. What to speak of the kids, when she is in a room even the adults avoid sitting there. There's Mausi, her school and her books, that is all. At school she must be scolding the children. Is that the way to live in a family? As if one part of a perfectly good body has gone dead or something, or like a tree all green and flourishing and just this one distinct branch still on the tree but all dried up.

Anna was in any case one big overgrown baby! At work, he was a foreman all right but at home he was a child, just as Baby and Ramu and Radha were. He laughs and talks like one, romps around like one and squabbles and fights like one. He has quarreled with Bhaskar several times, why they have even come to blows. If they are not children, what are they then? Sometimes it seems to me that they aren't just children, they are more than that, they are my children and I am not only their Akka - but their Amma too!

I remember the day I had scolded Mani Mama. Probably, even Amma would not have chided him so badly. But I hadn't been able to stop myself, I was helpless.

Baby had been away to Calcutta with Nana and he had written that she was returning to Jamshedpur with Mani Mama. That scared me – Baby and with Mani Mama! He is quite young, but age doesn't matter, it's just that he is really forgetful and totally irresponsible.

When Mama had come from Kolkata last time we had all been amazed to see him, so dreadfully cold and he wasn't even wearing a coat.

"Mama, don't you feel cold?" Bhaskar had asked.

"Of course I do!" His teeth were chattering.

"Why don't you wear a coat then?"

"I had," he laughed sheepishly, "but when I was asleep in the train some smart guy took it off me!"

Living in Kolkata, Mama spoke perfect Bengali just like all of us speak Hindi at home, Tamil we use only when we have guests from Chennai. But it wasn't his being a complete Bengali that surprised us. We were astonished at how he could sleep like the dead and not find out even when his coat was taken off him.

"Ticket?" Anna asked.

"That was in the pant pocket," Mama laughed, a Bengali sort of laugh.

But we hadn't believed him. That night when Mama slept off, Anna and Bhaskar had removed not only his shirt but also his vest, and Mama had slept through it all!

In the morning we all waited to see just how surprised he would be when he woke up. But he wasn't. He just laughed carelessly and said, "that's how yesterday in the train some fellow helped himself to my coat."

That's what Mani Mama is like! And Nana had sent Baby with him. If he slept off, any one could actually walk off with Baby and she was such a little thing, in any case.

The minute I saw Mama I was furious, "Mama, you are really stupid! Why did you bring Baby? What if you had lost her on the way?"

Mama didn't get angry. He smiled self-consciously. Scratching his neck he said softly, "I sat up all night in the train."

Then I was pacified. If Mama had slept off how would it have mattered, Baby was now home safe and sound! What can I do, I just worry too much. I am not the only one who thinks so, everyone in the family knows that I am like a mother to these children. Appa acknowledges this too.

I remember clearly that as soon as I had finished my B.A. Granny had told Appa that he should marry me off. "A grown up girl looks best in her husband's home" is how she had put it. How strange I had felt as if I had woken up for the first time. I had imagined all along that this was my home but actually it wasn't my home at all. Like a tree, my roots were entwined in every particle but this wasn't supposed to be my space. These roots, I'll have to gather them up, pull them out and shake them free from this earth. But then each particle would loosen, scatter and everything fall apart.

Anna heard this and was deeply irritated. "Who says Shyamali doesn't fit in here, we don't want any wedding! If she goes away who is going to feed us? When I have six o'clock duty who will wake me up, who will give me tea? Who will get the children ready and send then off to school?"

I saw three faces in front of me – Baby, Ramu and Radha, looking sort of wilted, unsure. As if trembling with fear, "Akka! You'll get married and go away?"

A lump formed in my throat. Taking each face gently in my hands, I wiped their tears, "don't worry, I'm not going anywhere, I'll be here with you."

Then I burst into tears and the three children were wiping away my tears, consoling me, "Akka! Akka! Don't cry Akka!"

Appa thought the whole thing over and he told Granny quite clearly that he could not marry me off yet, "when Raju (Anna) gets married and the children get a mother in the form of their eldest sister-in-law", only then could he think of my marriage.

Everyone was in high spirits that day. Anna was singing at the top of his voice, Bhaskar was chiding him, "listen Anna, you good for nothing fellow! Why are you bringing the roof down! Appa's built this house with his sweat and blood!" Anna didn't mind, he laughingly said, "Bhaskar, you fraud! How does it matter to your father if I'm bringing down the roof? It's my own dad's isn't it!"

Radha and Baby had called over their friends and were playing hop-scotch. Ramu was busy, persuading the newborn calf to read the newspaper, "come on read it I say, what if your mom is illiterate, utterly illiterate!"

Everything was truly festive at home that day. How delighted I myself was, like one feels when one escapes some awful punishment. And Appa was content in his children's happiness. For the first time in these last seven or eight years I had seen a faint hint of a gleam in Appa's eyes. Granny must have been fuming at Appa's stupidity, and Mausi was as detached as usual.

From then on our home was in a state of expectancy, a sense of waiting for a *bhabhi* for us, a wife for Anna and for Appa, a daughter-in-law. Anna never spoke of it but where was the need when all of us were busy getting him a wife.

The children were really enthusiastic. They were already drawing all sorts of plans. Which room would Anni occupy, who would say what to her, who would run errands for her and what each would gift her.

I was myself very eager to get a bhabhi. After all, the children had me, but who was there for me? Shouldn't there be an akka for me too, or an amma! What a sweet word – bhabi, Anni! Serene, caring, overflowing with love – that was my image of Anni! With open arms Anni had gathered all three children to her! The children were overjoyed and with a glowing face Anna too contemplated Anni – this picture left me elated, almost light hearted.

At times it seemed to me as if I was occupying someone else's place, working against a leave vacancy. The day the rightful occupant came I would be given leave.This didn't hurt me at all. I never felt any less important. Only the sense that I was indispensable until someone took my place. Till then I could not be spared, could not be given leave, could not be relieved.

Father brought home a photo one day. It caused quite a sensation at home. The photo was of our Anni. A wave of joy swept over us and then a tug of war. Anna wanted the picture for his wallet, Baby thought it should be in her trunk and Ramu wished that it were hung up on the wall, next to Shivji's photo. Ultimately it went into my album! No one objected to this, not Anna, not Baby, not even Ramu. I was after all their Akka!

The most precious thing at home those days was Anni's photo, and that was in my safe keeping because I was no less important than anyone else in the house. Every time we had a visitor, the first thing was to pull out the album and show them Anni's picture.

Excitement over the photo did dwindle but it didn't die out either. But there's no denying that it did become less important, after the day when with due pomp we brought Anni home with us. Anni was welcomed with great ceremony. Till the reception we were all madly busy but by then we found that Anni had become one of us. Our Anni, a tiny little thing, like a doll.

We showed Anni around our house, told her about the things there. About everybody's habits too. We talked of every possible thing. She listened to everything. She's really very sweet our Anni, speaks so affectionately to everyone.

Then Granny once again insisted that Shyamali should be married off, their *bahu* had come and she would now run the household.

"We will," Appa said, "she has only just come."

"When will you?" Granny scolded, "when the girl is an old maid! No one will marry her then, and what will she do here in this house then?"

Appa had to agree that it was time I got married. I felt I should prepare myself too. I began telling Anni everything about our home, as though I were handing over charge! She would listen carefully, "yes Akka! Yes Akka!"

It seemed a little strange to me. She was supposed to be my

eldest sister-in-law, meant to be not only my Anni but also in a way a mother to me, but she…

"Anni, you are my elder. Why do you call me Akka?"

Anni blushed, "I've got so much to learn from you. Even he has so much respect for you. How can I call you by name!"

I looked at Anni, my doll-like sweet little *bhabhi*! I could have taken her in my arms and hugged her to my heart's content, the way I do with Radha sometimes.

Just then from the drawing room we heard Anna and Bhaskar arguing loudly. Anni looked shocked, I just ignored it. They are at it all the time. Baby and Radha quarrel, then why shouldn't Anna and Bhaskar?

Ultilmately Anni and I went to the drawing room, "what is it Anna?"

"Look Shyamali!" Anna told me, "this wretch was sitting here reading his book, and the calf was standing here chewing away at the newspaper and he doesn't have a clue to what's going on!"

"So Bhaskar?" I turned towards Bhaskar.

Bhaskar's anger had perhaps vanished, "Ramu made him read the newspaper everyday, today he didn't. This little fellow probably strolled in to have a read. Why should I deny him his right to freedom of action!"

But Anna was not amused, not mollified. He thundered even louder, "as it is he has caused the damage and all he can do is joke. If the thug had to spend his own money, then it would be different."

"Oh shut up! You big Mr. Money Bags!" Now Bhaskar was furious too.

Both were locked together and I stood there and laughed. Anni forced them apart and stood aside shaking.

Just then Ramu sauntered past.

"If Anna beats up Bhaskar what can I do? Drink coffee?" he sang out.

I continued to laugh. Anni was still trembling. I felt a surge of tenderness for her, she is just like our Baby this Anni. Anyone quarrels and Baby is in tears.

But Anna's fury didn't subside and Appa was furious too. Neither of them showed up at dinnertime. "Won't you have dinner, Appa?" I went to call father.

"Has Ramu eaten?" he asked.

"What about Anna?"

"Tell him to eat!"

"Anna, come have your dinner," I called out to him.

"Tell Savitri to bring my food here."

I went off to look for Anni, but I felt odd. Anna had never done this before. Today perhaps they hadn't quarrelled like Radha and Baby do, the way children fight. Today for the first time, they had fought like adults!

Appa specially called me aside and told me to let Anni do all the housework now. I didn't see the point in putting our still new *bhabhi* to all this trouble. I was doing it all anyway, have been for so many years. I'm so used to it. I finish off all the work in the morning and go to the University, and rest in the evening when I get back, and at night I study. I have never felt that I can't manage all this, then why now? But Appa had told me to, so I left everything, I didn't do a thing that day.

The next day all the children were late for school. They couldn't help it. Anni wasn't able to get the food ready. It wasn't poor Anni's fault, she had never worked at home before. She did try very hard but it just got late. Poor thing wasn't used to rising early in the morning. She had been up from morning and she was now feeling sleepy and tired too.

To me it seemed that Appa had needlessly put this burden on her. I'm still around and can easily do the work, then...?

In the evening Appa called me, "Shyamali I want to talk to you."

"Anything special Appa?"

"Listen Shyamali!" Appa said, "I am not doing as fathers normally do. I know my daughter isn't a child anymore. She has grown up, is intelligent, educated, capable..."

"What is it Appa?" I said. Appa had never spoken to me like this before.

"I have found a match for you," Appa said, "he's an M.Sc. and working as a Scientific Officer. Think about it, and tell me what you feel."

Appa put a photo in my hands and walked off. A fair face, grey eyes, sharp features, it was an attractive photo. I don't know why I blushed even though I was alone... And that old feeling once again that this wasn't my home, that my place was somewhere else... where this man would be, I and my husband. Just the two of us...

Somehow I felt an outsider. Anyway Anni was now here, she would have to learn how to manage the home. The children wouldn't be late every day. It was only proper, there was no role here for me anymore. Good matches weren't that easy to find, get too old and getting married itself wouldn't be possible. And then, I know how dreary a single woman's life can be. Mausi's life was there for me to see – drab, barren, a burnt out desert without a trace of greenery anywhere.

Besides, the children had grown up too. Why, even Ramu's calf could read the newspaper...I broke into a smile.

Suddenly Anna was shouting in the drawing room, "you wretch! How dare you swear at me!"

I ran. It was just as I had feared. They fought not as children but as adults. There they were, the two of them facing each other... and Anni trembling there in the far corner, up against the wall.

"Anna! Bhaskar! What's wrong?" I scolded.

"Shyamali, don't you interfere today!" Bhaskar swore, "today I'm going to kill this bastard!" and he ran towards the cattle shed.

That they were hot-headed I knew. But did they hoard up all their anger only for each other? They had fought before, a hundred times and the whole neighbourhood would gather. How ashamed I would feel. But today it was altogether different.

Bhaskar returned with the chopper in his hand, "wretch, today I'll put an end to your bellowing."

"Come, come, chop me up if you dare!"

And I was shaking. Bhaskar had never picked up the chopper before. I clung on to him, "Bhaskar what's wrong! Leave it I say," and I snatched it from him.

But the two were locked together. Baby and Radha were there – both stood cowering in the corner and crying. Ramu too, but he didn't tease – "when Anna fought with Bhaskar then… what was I to do?" I held on to the two of them and shouted, "Anni, call Appa."

Appa had already come. He separated Anna and Bhaskar. But both continued to scream and abuse one another.

"Anna, please be quiet!" I said, "won't you listen to me?"

"Why is it always me you are after!" and he was angrier still, "why don't you tell this bastard to shut up!"

"Anna!" I was furious as well, "don't you care about me?"

"I don't care about anybody," Anna said.

I suddenly felt deflated as if the wind had gone out of my

sails. I retreated quietly to the kitchen. Baby, Radha and Ramu followed me, but I paid no attention to them.

Anna had never spoken to me in this way before. So he didn't care about me anymore. Why should he – he is grown up now, he had a wife now. Yes, why should he need me now! Sooner or later Bhaskar will get married and he won't need me either. Ramu will bring a wife too. Baby and Radha will go off with their husbands. And who will be left – Appa and I. Appa, he has lived his life, but what about me? I will stay on in this family – like Mausi, like the dried out branch of a tree, or a dead worthless limb! When no one needs me any longer, what will I do then? I will be middle-aged by then and well beyond getting married. That Scientific Officer in the photo, he will belong to another and here will be Anna's wife, Bhaskar's and Ramu's wives, their children, and I – barren land, existing here like Mausi.

But why should I stay on like this? Tomorrow I will tell Appa, as soon as I've finished my M.A. you can marry me off. When no one needs me, why should I stay on? I too will go away to a home of my own…

Anna and bhabhi stayed in their own room. Bhaskar had most probably gone out somewhere. The children were asleep while Appa was pacing around his room. I don't think anyone had eaten. How could anyone when no one had cooked. And I lay around on my bed, planning how I would leave for my own home along with that Scientific Officer.

When I woke up next morning Ramu was sitting on the edge of my bed, "Akka"…

"What is it?" I was puzzled.

"Akka!" Ramu looked at me with tear-filled eyes, "Akka, I'm hungry," and he clung on to me.

"Oh my poor little brother! A curse on your Akka! What use is your Akka if she is around and you remain hungry!"

"Akka," he sobbed in a small voice, "Akka, Baby and Radha are crying. They are hungry too."

I jumped up – these poor children! No one has given them anything to eat since last night. What will become of them if I go away, who will care for them? If Anna doesn't need me, why should he need them? And if Anna doesn't care, then why would Anni trouble herself!

I went to the kitchen. Ramu was close behind. Baby and Radha, I saw, had silently entered and were looking expectantly at me. Their cheeks were tear-stained. My hands worked at a furious pace.

Briskly I made a rice batter, put oil on the *tava* and began making *dosas*. The batter sizzled on the *tava* and their eyes were fixed hungrily on the *dosa*. A smile appeared on Ramu's face. How much Ramu resembles Anna! It seemed as if it was Anna smiling at me. Ramu ... Anna! Anna doesn't need me now, tomorrow neither will Ramu, but today... Ramu is hungry, Baby and Radha are hungry... I'll not leave. I'll stay on – right here, in this house ... for them... but tomorrow when Ramu no longer needs me... it'll be too late for me to marry ... my life will then be Mausi's life... a dry branch, a dead limb ... what then should I tell Appa? Let me think ... what answer do I give that Scientific Officer? What shall I do?

And before me sit Baby, Radha and Ramu, and they are hungry... Ramu looks like Anna, when he smiles, it seems to me as if Anna is smiling!

IDENTITY

Is he conscious?" I asked.

"He's been conscious since yesterday."

There was not a trace of joy in his voice as he told me, only an extraordinary tiredness.

Momentarily, I was blank. He was conscious, yet Anil was unhappy. There had to be some other reason for his anxiety.

"General condition?"

"The doctor's say it's okay."

Simply words. His tone gave no reason for me to hope that he was actually well.

"Blood pressure? Heart condition?"

"Everything is normal, they say."

"Reflexes?"

"They're okay."

What else could it be? Left with no alternative I decided to ask him, "why then are you so dejected?"

The infinite anguish in his eyes troubled me deeply, "he doesn't recognise me."

I was stunned – what could this be: had he lost his memory or was there some mental disorder?

"Why?" I asked.

"Don't know."

"Does he recognise anyone else?"

"Whether he recognises the doctors and nurses or not, how does it matter."

At a loss, I gazed at him. What could I say?

Suddenly, his hands came alive. He restlessly stroked his forehead as though his fingers were itching to tear his hair out. He rubbed his palms, his cheeks, his chin – he was perhaps trying to keep himself from crying… for his eyes were already moist. Undoubtedly he was worried and miserable to find his father unable to recognise him, his one and only child, in fact the only person in this world he could call his own. His son, the one who had brought him at great expense to this exclusive hospital, one who was known by the entire nation, and who was bound someday to be hailed by the whole world. His own father failed to recognise him.

We were both seated in the Holy Family Hospital's second floor lobby, just outside his cabin. A cool moist breeze flowed from the open window behind us. Normally, Delhi is lovely only in October and February. But occasionally, the last week of July also turns delightful. It was raining, but just a fine drizzle, enough to cool a man but not wet him. Just wet enough to wash nature but not turn her muddy. Incredibly fresh greenery all around, the sky overcast and the trees swaying in the damp breeze like an enticing young woman. Why wouldn't Delhi be enchanting…

The mind couldn't linger on the breeze indefinitely. The staircase was before us and next to it, the lift. The rest were rooms, rows and rows of them. Endless corridors or rather, lanes. Lanes is what they seemed to me… There's no other hospital in Delhi as neat and tidy as this. And here, to the left, in the cabin next to the waiting room, was where Anil's father was lying. He had had some sort of a fit and had become unconscious. He had been brought unconscious to the hospital, and now Anil was telling me that he had become conscious, but was unable to recognise him…

The lift stopped and swinging his stethoscope, out stepped a doctor.

"Dr. Bhatia!" Anil said and stood up, "may be he's come to see father!"

His eyes seemed to be asking me if he could go…

"Go speak to the doctor," I said.

To be near his father and get information from the doctors: this was clearly his most urgent task. Yet he moved from there, as though in leaving me, he was guilty of a heinous crime. His eyes, his lips, the lines on his face… if it hadn't looked so ridiculous, he would I am pretty sure, have folded his hands before me to ask permission.

Anil is much too sensitive! Savoring each mood to its very conclusion – as if he must penetrate to the essence of each thing. No wonder there's such depth in his paintings. Even the mountains in his paintings seem to speak! It seems as if his eyes simply refuse to stop at the surface of things – they must search, pierce through every layer, to lay bare the soul itself…

……………………………………

We must have been in the fourth standard at that time. The two of us used to sit in the front row and talk of just about everything. But, even as we talked, the pen in his hand was perpetually busy. He would sketch endlessly in his drawing book or ordinary exercise book or a piece of paper or anything that lay before him. I even saw him a couple of times, drawing on the wooden desk in front of him…. His pen was never idle and from it, flowed an ever changing, endless stream of visions! Sometimes it would be a mountain with a river flowing at its base and a cloud-hidden sky with the sun or moon shining through.

Otherwise, a desert scene – a couple of chador trees, a spring and travellers seated on camels or else, the seashore – waves, coconut palms and people…

I would walk away or listen to him or simply watch as those scenes appeared magically from his pen… For me he was not mere artist but a magician, a wizard, who at every moment scattered from his pen enchanted worlds before me. If on occasion, with great fanfare I sat down to draw, not even after a hundred efforts I could get a line straight. Many a time I would copy his scenes but my mountain would scarcely look like a mountain or the palm like a palm! As for him, a few strokes of the pen and dynamic, living forms would emerge: neither pencil nor eraser… and the picture would be done. If any teacher arrived for class, he would quietly crumble the paper. It hurt me to see such a callous destruction of his pictures. So I finally told him, he could give me any he didn't want…

That morning, when I reached school he was busy drawing in his book.

"What're you making?" I asked, and putting down my lunch-box, I looked eagerly at the picture. It wasn't one of his usual landscapes – mountains, deserts or seashores. It was altogether different. A vast crossing. A fountain and garden to one side, and a road in the front winding into the distance. Towering buildings and beds of flowers everywhere…

"What's this?" I asked

"Vijay Chowk," he said. "It's very pretty. I went yesterday right up to India Gate. That's what I'm making."

Today he was in no mood to talk. He was completely absorbed in the drawing before him.

When the bell rang that day, he didn't crush and crumble the page, he carefully smoothed out the paper, stroking it lovingly with his hand and put it away inside his book.

The next four periods passed, but he had time only to open his book and look again and again at that incomplete picture. There was no way that he could complete it. As soon as the bell rang for the break, out came the book and his pen flew over the page. He talked as well but not in his usual way. I knew his focus was entirely on the drawing.

And then the break ended and the bell for the fifth period rang.

All at once his face was transformed by fear. He looked at the picture and then gazed anxiously out of the door. Was the teacher on his way … then he looked at me, "I'm going, I have to finish this picture."

Before I could quite understand his intention, he had already gathered his books, stuffed them into his bag, and left the room. Stunned, I stared at the empty door.

What he had in his mind I do not know. What I knew was that he should finish the picture as quickly as he could and not crumble and throw it away as he usually did. Let him give it to me. I would ask my father to get it framed and I would hang it up in my room.

Sadhuram Sharma, our maths teacher, arrived at this precise moment. He looked at the empty seat.

"Hasn't Anil come today?"

"He came sir!" some of the boys chimed.

"Then where has he gone?"

Total silence. How could anyone know where he had gone? Even I knew only that he had left the class, but where he had gone…?

"All of you wait here. Let me get the register…"

Attendance at our school was taken only in the first period. But in exceptional cases the register was sent for and once again the attendance was checked. Not to come to school at all was common enough, but to vanish like this was a most shocking crime.

That's exactly what happened. Sadhuram Sharma returned from the office, register in hand. Attendance was called again. Everyone else was present, Anil was the only one missing. In bold red letters Sadhuram Sharma wrote 'FLED' before his name. He had barely closed his pen and put it away in his pocket when Hariprasad, the school peon, came into the room, clutching Anil by the arm and dragging him behind.

Chasing a cow from the school compound, a gardener had found Anil. He was sitting in a remote corner of the playground, under a vast shady tree, busy completing his drawing. He had caught Anil and marched him to the headmaster who had sent him here.

They wrote in his diary that he had run away from his maths class and was found sitting outside, drawing. He was told to get the note signed by his father.

Somehow the last three periods of the day passed. When school was over, I couldn't help myself, "Anil, will you give me this drawing?"

"It isn't even finished yet," he said getting up from his seat.

"When it's done will you give it to me?"

"No!" He told me bluntly, "I'll complete it and give it to my papa! If he likes it I'll give it to him, otherwise I'll keep it carefully for myself."

The next day I asked him eagerly, "have you finished it?"

He grimaced, "no!"

"Why? What happened? You didn't get the time?"

" No!" He was crestfallen. "Papa gave me a good thrashing when I told him what happened at school. He tore up the unfinished picture. He warned me that if he ever found out that I was drawing pictures again, he would break every single bone in my body." I had never ever seen Anil so dejected.

"Why doesn't papa understand what I'm saying? I'm not one of those worthless kids who run away from school to escape their lessons. I know studies are important. I'm studying in any case and will go on studying ... but drawing..."

....

Dr. Bhatia had come out of the cabin, but Anil was not with him. I felt like stopping him and asking how Anil's father was doing. Perhaps, he didn't want to tell Anil the whole truth. After all, now that he had regained consciousness, why was he not recognising his only son?

Dr. Bhatia walked past me but I didn't get up. I didn't speak. I just sat there thinking. This often happens with me: my mind keeps thinking but my body doesn't stir from its place... Dr. Bhatia had vanished into the lift.

I got up.

For a moment I hesitated at the cabin door. There wasn't a sound from within. What was Anil doing inside? ... flirting with a nurse...?

Opening the door I went in. No nurse was in the cabin. Anil's father was asleep, and his chair pulled up right next to the bed, sat Anil. He was holding his father's wrist and trying it seemed, to find his pulse. From the look on his face it was clear that he could not. It was ironic that Anil the artist, so acutely sensitive to the slightest change in society's moods, his hand responsive to the pulse of human emotion, could not locate the heartbeat in his father's inert form!

For a moment I stood close to him.

Raising his head he looked at me.

"Can't find it?" I asked mechanically.

"No!" and he stared again at his father's closed eyes.

I looked around the room: it was a spacious bedroom-like a cabin, air-conditioned. Apart from the bed, there was a table and a couple of chairs in the corner. A stand for clothes and a sideboard too…

There was no shortage of money for Anil these days… but things weren't like this for Anil's folks when we were in school. His father was the Assistant Postmaster in the local post office and he couldn't have dreamt of being treated in an air-conditioned cabin of this hospital…

Anil had got fifty five percent in the Matric Exam. He hadn't really expected more than that. We had gone together to college and filled out the forms for the Intermediate course. Anil had told me that his father had wanted him to take admission in the commerce class.

"Why?" I asked.

"He thinks it will be easier to get a job. Literature and philosophy is what I want to study. I don't want to be a clerk or an accountant," he had said.

"But what about a job?"

"Where's the need for a job," he laughed. "Long live my brushes!"

The conflict at home had gone on for a long time. His father had stubbornly insisted that he change his subjects and equally obstinate, he had stood firm. He had categorically declared that if he was forced to do B.Com., he would abandon his studies.

It was the last week of August, I think. The Independence Day celebrations in college were just over. He hadn't come to college for the last two days. Could be that he was sick…

Two nurses walked in with a large tray full of things. Smiling they looked at the two of us, "we have to sponge the patient."

I left the room immediately, as if I was desperate to get out. I was just waiting for an opportunity to escape. Perhaps being in the company of an unconscious person had unnerved me.

As soon as I sat down in the lobby I admitted to myself that I was afraid. And yet, I was also deeply ashamed of myself. Why should I be so panic-stricken. Shouldn't we minister the sick or should we feel afraid and run away from them like children? Anyone can fall sick. As it is, I had come prepared to stay all night at the hospital with Anil. What of that? If I was going to lose my nerve like this how could I be of any help?

Anil too came out of the room.

"I'm just going out for an hour," he said, "I'll bring dinner when I come. We'll have it together."

"Fine."

"When the nurses have done with the sponging you sit inside, near papa," he said. "There's nothing to be nervous about. If you need anything, just ring the bell, the nurse will come."

I nodded my head silently and he disappeared downstairs. Anil had always avoided using the lift. For a couple of floors, he would go up the stairs and for going down he had never used the lift, even if he had ten floors to cross.

As he went out of sight I lapsed once more into a reverie. But the past didn't go away. Like an old worn out reel of film, it played before my eyes.

...I had gone over to Anil's place to find out why he wasn't to be seen. There I discovered that his family too were looking for him. He had enrolled in college with the rest of us, his mother told me, but he wasn't happy about it. He had gone to the College of Art and brought all their forms and things. It was inconceivable for his father to agree to his joining the Art College. He could at least become a clerk after his B.A. but what would he do with a diploma in painting? Probably sit on the roadside or footpath, and paint signboards for shopkeepers. To visualise a condition better that this for a painter, was completely beyond his imagination.

There had been a bitter quarrel between father and son. Now, for the last two days, he had been missing from home. God knows where he was. I had come to ask them about Anil and here they were prodding me to know where he had gone.

I was feeling pretty rotten. I had thought that he couldn't hide anything from me while all the time he didn't let me have the faintest idea of what was going on inside him…

Later, when we met, he told me how after seeing one of his drawings, a teacher from the College of Art had taken him under his wing. His fees had been waived, and they had given him a room in the hostel. When his father had hunted for him all over town, he could not have imagined that Anil was safely lodged in a hostel room, free of cost.

A few days later, he had come home on his own. He had again told his father that if he weren't allowed to study a course of his choice, he would leave home and never come back.

I do not know what actually happened amongst them at home. Apparently things seemed to have been patched up. He stayed on in the hostel, but came home every once in a while. Whenever we met, he would laugh and say, "Papa still hasn't forgiven this good for nothing son of his!"

……………………………………

"You can now go in," said the nurse, coming out of the cabin.

Silently, I entered.

Anil's father was awake and conscious. He opened his eyes once and as though there was nothing before him, he shut them again.

For reasons I could not understand, this time I was unable to return to the past. Anil was not there, I was alone with his father and had to look after him. Placing a chair near his bed I sat down. At the sound of the chair, he again opened his eyes. The blankness of his eyes however was unchanged, even though I was sitting just there in front of him.

His indifference towards me kindled a sharp desire to communicate with him. My fears somehow disappeared and I spontaneously put my hand on his forehead. Yet again his eyes opened.

"Uncle! Do you recognise me?"

There was no reaction at all, as if I had not spoken at all... He neither smiled in acknowledgement nor brushed me aside in irritation. I saw neither a shadow of recognition in his eyes, nor the faintest echo of a sound from his throat.

He shut his eyes again.

I was not as hurt as Anil had been. His failure to recognise me did not upset me in the least. In a spirit of complete detachment, I simply accepted the fact that while the eyes are merely the tools of vision, it is the intellect that must empower them to see.

He drifted into sleep as effortlessly as we blink our eyes.

The present was merely a state of boredom. It had nothing to offer. Seated on that chair I tried to sleep though the mind slipped back into the past.

....

Anil had recounted to me how his father had slowly reconciled to his choice of art. He had even begun to take an interest in his subjects. He now knew that there were two streams in the art course – commercial and fine art. Anil was really happy that his father was involved in how he was doing, what his future plans were and the possibility of an independent career for him.

What Papa already knew about his studies ultimately proved disastrous for Anil. In the final year, when he was selecting 'fine art' as his specialisation, his father wanted him to opt for commercial art so that he could get a job in an advertising agency.

In his four years of study, Anil had become not just a skilled painter but an artist as well. We often went out together, and I had seen him produce a dozen sketches even as we waited at a bus stop. His pen was like the legendary horn of plenty, spilling out image after image. He would look for barely a moment and before you knew, there was the image on paper: the man's appearance, his shape and temperament, his expressions and feelings; why, even his entire personality… Anil wasn't just a painter, he was an x-ray machine! Nothing escaped his eye or his pen. And when he used his brush, he drew not just the forms but the also soul of things…and all along, while he worked at his technique, he was developing his own independent philosophy of art. Steadily he grew in stature as an artist and thinker. "What is art", "what role should it play in human development?", "what is its relation to religion?" He could speak for hours on questions such as these. In his canvases, the subtle relationship between human images and natural settings expressed his own unique vision of life.

And papa was adamant he specialise in commercial art! This was his final effort to salvage his son's future!

But the artist in Anil had risen to heights from which he was no longer willing to descend. This time round, the altercations between father and son had been particularly bitter. The son's growing self-confidence was matched by the father's senility.

Anil then stopped coming home. All contact with his parents

ceased. Things came to such a pass that when Anil left for further studies in Rome and Paris, no effort to meet was made by either side.

The cabin door creaked.

Anil had returned.

"Papa's sleeping?" he asked.

"Yes, he's been sleeping." Rising, I went near him.

"He didn't wake up at all?"

"He woke up for a while after the sponging but fell off to sleep again."

"Did he speak to you?"

"No."

He couldn't have looked more disappointed even if his most outstanding paintings had been viewed without a single comment.

"Come, let's have dinner," he said after a while.

He had brought many things. In fact, he converted the corner table into a regular dining room with plates and cutlery.

Silently we ate. Father lay in the sleep of the unconscious while the son was lost in a peculiar weariness. What then was there for me to say.

... In this silence of the present I turned once more to the past.

....

No doubt when he left for Europe, Anil broke all ties with his parents. But on his return to India, at the time of his marriage, both sides had earnestly tried not just to resume contact, but to actually bridge the gulf of years.

His father was eager to restore their relationship so that he could find, from his own community, a suitable bride for him, and Anil was equally keen for the contact, so that Emily would have their blessings. But neither succeeded. Father didn't get the daughter-in-law of his choice, nor Emily their blessings!

Yes, the eagerness on both sides had certainly succeeded in further widening the gap.

After that, only once had Anil gone home, and that too, alone. That was when his mother had died…

Now perhaps, his father lay dying. I emerged again from the past into the present.

Lost in his thoughts, Anil had eaten nothing.

"I say, you're not taking anything," I reminded him. My words acted like a probe. How strange was his look: like one of his own paintings, the portrait of an immeasurably sad old man.

"What's happened to you?" I whispered.

"Nothing." He rose pushing away his plate, "Terrible! Papa just isn't able to identify me…"

That was it! His words made something inside me snap. I felt like angrily asking him, "did your papa ever identify you, your whole life?"

But then, I checked myself. He was already painfully unhappy… besides, I really wasn't sure which identity he was speaking of…

THE SPLINTER

After three days of incessant rain, the sun had finally appeared. The clouds had scattered, the sky was clear, and the sunshine felt wonderful.

For the last couple of days, Lithi Khuang had not been well at all. The sunshine did her a world of good. Of course, one couldn't say for sure if it was the weather. Maybe she was actually feeling better.

Her husband Ho had been away from morning. He had been able to set out only because the weather had cleared.

She had seen him off and was busy pottering around the house. She was keen to finish off all the housework before he returned around midday. Then the two of them could spend this golden day peacefully together.

In their little settlement, just outside the town of Hin Hua, in the Ha Bok province of Vietnam, such golden days were really quite rare. Li pined for such days. For some time now she was filled with a keen desire to do certain things: like visit a particular place, eat some specific thing. Two years ago, when she was pregnant for the first time, she had felt such cravings. But her desires had been quite different then. Her appetite for sweets had been enormous, now Li fancied only sour. That time it had been a boy and Li simply knew that this time it would be a girl.

These days, without any warning, Li was often engulfed by tenderness. She felt she was already the mother of two. She carried within herself a double quota of warmth. She couldn't quite love her unborn daughter yet, but sometimes when alone, she gently stroked her swollen belly. So she caressed her as yet unseen, unknown daughter and even talked to her. And when the kicking inside became too vigorous, she gently chided her for being naughty, "why do you trouble me, my little one! If you are this playful now, what will you be up to once you are born! No, my baby, good little girls don't trouble their mothers," she would explain.

And she would smile to herself, a private little smile.

For the rest, she would lavish all her love on her son.

Today, right from the morning she had been busy with her son. She felt annoyed sometimes, and wondered that she had nothing better to do all day than look after father and son. Little Kai was really much too naughty and wouldn't listen to her at all.

The sunshine made her feel that she should bathe Kai. What with the constant rain, she hadn't bathed him for the last two days. He could easily have caught a cold. She had to do it today. He was now looking far too dirty, and one never knew what the weather might be like tomorrow!

Li had put everything she needed in the courtyard and had even managed to catch hold of Kai. He just refused to stop bawling. Caged indoors for the last three days, today he wanted to frisk around, play in the dirt and even run outside the compound. He certainly didn't want to sit still and get a bath, she too felt like letting him play for a while. But once he ran off, she would never be able to catch hold of him again. It was already late enough and if she didn't hurry, Ho would be back and her work still not done.

"No, my little boy, you mustn't cry," she soothed, "come, come, it isn't that bad! Don't tire out your mother so," she admonished.

Kai kept on wailing and Li kept peeling off his clothes. Off came his shirt. Next his vest, and then he threw such a tantrum, that he almost slipped out of her grasp. Li just about managed to drag him back. Clutching him firmly she tested the water with her free hand – no, it wasn't too cold.

And just then, there was this vigorous movement inside her.

Li placed her wet hand on her stomach. "No, my little one, no!" she cooed, "don't trouble me, let me bathe your brother."

There was Kai howling wildly and straining to get free, and here was this …Li smiled as she looked at her swollen stomach. "Naughty children! Both of you, brother and sister, are bent on vexing me!"

And then she thought that if Ho had been at home, he would surely have helped her.

The baby was kicking ever more strongly. She won't stay in here much longer, she told herself.

Turning to Kai, she poured a mug of water over his head. He cried even louder.

She rubbed soap all over his hair. I'll soap his face later, she thought, as she worked at the dirt on his hands.

There was a vigorous quivering inside her. Then suddenly, this loud roaring. Li wondered what had happened to the baby….?

That very instant she knew it wasn't the baby at all. It was the sky that was humming, and with it came a cloud of smoke and dust, a foul curtain that covered the blue sky and filthied the air. And flying through this noxious haze, was a formation of five aeroplanes.

She knew at once. Clutching the soap-covered Kai to herself, her other hand supporting the little one growing inside her, she ran towards the house.

Water, soap, towel and mug all lay as they were, scattered, abandoned, exposed.

Noise everywhere. Fire and smoke. The earth belching mud and dirt from its entrails, up into the sky. And the red fire, it rained down again upon the earth.

The explosions moved even closer, and seemed to Li to surround her house. And here she was, alone at home, with her two little children, each naughtier than the other.

All at once, the courtyard erupted. Soap and towel, bucket and water disappeared into the smoke. And sprawled in the middle of the room fell Li with Kai still in her arms.

An agonised shriek tore from Li's throat followed. It was like a sword that ripped through her buttock and burrowed deeper and deeper inside.

Kai fell silent. He slipped from her arms, and covered in soap and mud sat there before her.

Tears welled up with the unbearable pain. She bit her lower lip. Sinking her teeth into her lip, she wanted to cut it, tear it, do anything to forget the pain in her buttock.

Outside, the drone of the planes had faded into the distance.

Pressing her stomach with her right hand she moved the left onto her buttock. She felt the naked flesh – no cloth there anymore – and a warm sticky fluid coated her hand.

She brought her hand before her eyes and saw that it was blood.

Again she bit her lip, to deaden the pain. Moving her arms and legs she tried to scramble up, only to slip and fall back. And Kai sat there besides her, crying desperately.

Ho was at the fringes of their settlement when he heard the hum of the aeroplanes. This was a familiar enough sound for him. By now they had grown accustomed to it. This war had dragged on for years, and would go on for how many more years, no one knew.

Every couple of days, planes would arrive out of nowhere, just as they had done today. They would drop their bombs and then, beyond their homes, Hin Hua would be shrouded in dust and smoke.

For the last three days, rains had kept the planes away. Now that the sun was out, they too were back…

He didn't know what he was to do. One thing was clear. At a time like this, he should have been at home with Li and Kai. So far, not a single bomb had fallen on their homes - but if planes continued to appear in this fashion, it could happen any day.

Bombs had begun falling suddenly: explosions, fire and smoke all around. Nothing visible anywhere. Ho lay flat on the ground. There was no sense of time. When had the planes arrived, when had the bombs rained down, when had the planes gone away, he could not tell. A single question filled his mind: were Li and Kai okay?

Sensing that the planes were no longer overhead, he scrambled up and ran.

His heart was pounding. Today was the first time they had been directly hit – God have mercy on us all!

He was racing through the slowly scattering smoke.

There were no more explosions, but the noise around had grown. Screams and cries from every house. Volunteers and officials were on the scene. Vehicles dashing about in all directions.

When he saw his house, he thought his heart would stop. The bomb had fallen in his courtyard. A scream broke from him and he raced inside, tears streaming down his cheeks.

Lying before him, covered in blood, was Li. At her head sat Kai, crying.

Ho kneeled by her, "Li! Li!"

No answer from Li.

Kai saw his father and cried even louder.

Ho looked around helplessly. There was no one. Trying to turn Li over onto her back, his hand touched the turbulence within her body...

He just did not know what to do!

At that moment an officer, along with a few volunteers, swarmed into the house. With trembling lips and eyes brimming with tears, Ho stood and watched.

The official knew at once what had happened. Bending down he turned Li over and checked her heartbeat. Looking up at the others, "she's alive'" he said.

Stooping down, the volunteers picked up Li and carried her out.

Weeping, Ho took Kai into his arms and followed behind.

They laid Li in the ambulance with the four or five wounded who were already in there. He climbed into the other jeep. Kai stopped crying and looked around with fear-filled eyes. Everything was done automatically. Not a word had been spoken.

The jeep set off and the ambulance followed. They headed off towards Hin Hua. Did they think Li was just another of the wounded, or did they know that inside her was a tiny being eager to see the light of day? With Li in this state, did the fragile creature have any chance?

Ho wanted desperately to get up and tell the officer this. But everyone else was so silent. Besides, in his present state he wondered if he could utter a single intelligible sound.

The sun had already set. The convoy entered the hospital compound and he still hadn't told the official anything at all.

Ho paced from one corner of the verandah to the other. All night he had walked up and down and now dawn had begun to stain the sky red.

He had no recollection at all how the night had passed. All he knew was that after one brisk look at Li, the doctor had sent her straight to the operating theatre. He had been told that Li had been hit by the scattering shrapnel. One splinter had pierced her left buttock and was lodged deep inside. They would operate to remove it. Li was shut inside the theatre and he kept vigil outside.

Kai lay asleep on the bench. He looked at him rolled up into a tight bundle. If only he could cover him with a sheet. But where could he get a sheet here!

He had walked all night. No one had told him how Li was. Would she even make it - he had no idea. What if she died?

"Let me speak to her for a while before she dies," he wanted to say. But to whom? Was there anyone here who would listen to him? They had taken his Li behind that door and no one had let him go in. He did not even have the courage to walk in on his own.

And just then the door opened.

Ho turned around and stood still, struggling to breathe.

"Mr. Ho! You can come in now," the nurse in the doorway said.

She had led him winding through the corridors to the ward. In that jungle of beds full of the wounded, he saw Li.

She was alive. But tears were streaming from her eyes. One loud heart-rending sob when she saw Ho, and then she lapsed, as before into silent tears.

A heavy load was off his mind. His lips broke into a smile. "Li! Why are you crying?"

He came and stood near her pillow. Not a word did she speak. Puzzled, he looked at her and then turned to the nurse.

The nurse had moved next to him. "We are sorry Mr. Ho! We could not save your daughter."

"Daughter!" And then Ho remembered the little creature Li had been carrying inside her.

His eyes suddenly swam with tears.

"Would you like to see the baby?" the nurse was asking him.

Mechanically he nodded his head. He trailed behind her through a maze of corridors, till he found himself standing in front of a door.

Gesturing for him to wait outside, the nurse went in.

He stood staring at this door. Beyond it was his daughter. Till yesterday she had still been a part of Li's body.

The door opened. In her arms was a baby, wrapped in a white cloth. She lifted the cloth aside.

A healthy, pretty baby lay in the folds. Its face was wrinkled into a cry. Perhaps his little girl had died crying her heart out.

Turning the baby's head, the nurse showed him her left cheek. There, on the cheek was this fresh livid wound. The skin was torn and the naked red flesh shone through. Around it, the dried blood was just turning black.

"That splinter in your wife's buttock," she said, "that's what did this."

She covered the baby with the cloth.

"We are truly sorry, Mr. Ho!" she said again, "we could not save your daughter. But such a tiny wounded creature - we have never handled one before, you see."

The nurse shut her eyes and let the tears roll down her cheeks. She walked back inside.

A short while later, Ho was seated on a stool by Li's bedside. Kai sat on his lap, a puzzled look on his face. He gazed, sometimes at his mother and then turned to look at his father. Not a word was uttered. There was only silence.

MY OWN WORLD

The train suddenly began to slow down. Maybe a station was approaching, maybe not. Someone may have pulled the chain, or the signal may be red. There may not be enough coal or water perhaps, or some part may have failed, or maybe some other train was coming on the same track. Anything could happen when I was on this train, I felt. Well, something may or may not have happened, but the train certainly slowed down.

I sat up. Mother was lying with her eyes shut. She must have got tired. For one who struggled to walk even a dozen steps, the overnight journey may have drained her. Mother was sick. Till this day I hadn't been able to comprehend her sickness. No two doctors could agree on what was wrong. Either she suffered from something that the doctors couldn't fathom, or every disease existing in the world had found a home in her system. Or perhaps, it was just old age, the most dreadful disease of all.

I checked our baggage and counted the items. Everything was in order. Nothing had been lost, and despite the tediously lengthy journey, nothing was stolen. And here I was, quite unable to believe it. For the last twenty four hours, I'd agonised that something may go wrong. There'd be some disaster, something may happen to me or to the luggage. But nothing went wrong. Somewhere deep within I was still afraid, but good sense made me accept this comforting truth.

Reassured, I looked out of the window.

The train had crossed the Yamuna bridge and begun to enter the station. The poles that bristled around the platforms were being left behind one by one. The panting, wheezing sound of the engine, which had distressed me all the way, was calmed. Its carefree, chugging tones were now filled with the joy of reaching home!

I too felt a certain kind of joy. At least the journey was done. We hadn't got much space at night and the whole body was stiff with sitting. Now, at last, we would get some rest. But at the same time, an unknown fear grabbed me. Like a fish in water, this fear had started diving and surfacing and diving again, in my mind. What if Sarla's brother was not at the station? Or, even if he were, suppose he couldn't find us or failed to recognise us? I'd never met him. What would happen? Where would the two of us go in this huge city? I did not know anyone here...

I felt angry at my stupidity. What was the sense of coming to a strange, unknown city without knowing anyone? I should at least have waited to hear from Sarla's brother before setting out. I should have let him confirm that he'd got news of our arrival and would meet us at the station. Or should have taken a contact number of some place where we could have gone, if necessary. If he didn't show up, I could still go to stay at a hotel, but what if in my ignorance, I landed up at some undesirable place?

The wheels let out squeals of protest and the train came to a halt with a jerk.

As daylight dawned and passengers began to get down at the last couple of stations, there had finally been some space in the compartment. Mother had been lying down quietly with her eyes closed. The jerk made her open her eyes. "Kavita, has the station come?"

"Yes mother, it has."

There was no sense in either mother's question or in my

answer. One could see that the station had come. There was plenty of activity on the platform. Unbearable noise and confusion. People milling around everywhere. A typical railway station, just like they show in Hindi films. And right in the middle of all this frantic activity, I stood absolutely still, like a stone. What could I do? It was after all the first time that I'd come like this to an unknown city.

"Do you need a *coolie*, *behenji*?"

I looked up. A *coolie* was standing in the doorway. It hadn't occurred to me that we'd need a *coolie*. Just as well, this fellow had shown up or there'd have been one more worry on my mind.

Taken by surprise, I blurted out, "Yes, take down the luggage."

The *coolie* came into the compartment. He took down my battered trunk as mother, seated on the lower berth, looked tentatively at me and then the *coolie*. "Mother, come!" and I caught mother by the arm to make her get up. Taking tiny steps, she made her way slowly to the door. Stepping down onto the platform, I held her by her hand and helped her climb down. The coolie followed us with the baggage. "Where do we have to go?" he asked.

That's exactly what I had been wondering, but he'd hardly understand. Still, I had to say something, "someone is coming to receive us."

I stopped. What does 'someone' mean? What could he make of it? Suppose I were to say 'he' is to come? I looked up to see his reaction…

"*Behenji*, should I go to the waiting room?" My words hadn't affected him at all. How did it matter to him whether we were to be received or not? All he wanted was to dump our luggage wherever and take his money and leave.

If we went to the waiting room, how would Sarla's brother know he should look for us there? And, in the ladies waiting room, who would let him enter? How foolish I'd look hanging around near the door waiting for some stranger whom I neither knew nor recognised. It would be best if we stayed right where we were. If he came to the station, he would at least check out all the people on the platform.

"No, just wait here for a while," very hesitantly I said.

"How can I wait, *memsahib*!" His tone and his mode of address changed. "I've got to find another load to carry. How can we feed our kids if we carry just one bunch of stuff from one train. Surely you know how costly things have become…"

The anger in his tone stung me. But given the situation, what else could I do? I couldn't pay him for two loads – there were plenty of things in the market that I found far too expensive and there was nothing I could do to reduce the prices for him or for myself either… I had to wait. I didn't want to go anywhere while he was insisting on taking the luggage somewhere, as long as his job was done. I began to feel stressed.

"That's alright." I had no idea what I was going to say to him.

"Listen, you…"

I had forgotten in this squabble that mother was also with me and could also help out. Just then, there was an unknown voice at my elbow.

Turning, I saw someone standing nearby. Dressed in a white pant and shirt, he wore pale coloured goggles that were much too big for his eyes but looked stylish. Whether he was a boy or a man, I could not quite decide. He had a little of both in his features and I think, he did resemble Sarla.

"You're Sarla's brother?" I spoke without any deliberate thought.

"Yes!" he smiled confidently, "and you must be Kavitaji?"

"Yes!"

The uncertainty that had unsettled me so much till now was completely gone. A huge load slid off my mind and I felt body and spirit visibly relax. He'd come, there was nothing to fear.

I had a good look at him. Then introduced Ma, "this is my mother".

He folded his hands and greeted us silently. Mother didn't raise hers but she was mumbling something under her breath, words of blessing I suppose. She must have been relieved to see my worries subside with his arrival.

"Please come! *Coolie*, let's go."

The *coolie* had not spoken a word since his arrival. Now, quietly picking up the luggage, he set off. We had to walk the entire length of the platform, to make our way to the exit beyond the sprawling hall. On our right were the booking counters and on the other side, the inquiry counter and benches. The hall itself, with hoards of people, resembled an extremely untidy house with things scattered everywhere.

The *coolie* was racing ahead. Mother was lagging behind. And he, walked just behind the *coolie*, and ahead of us. There hadn't been any more conversation since he came. Walking silently like this made me uneasy. He'd come to receive me, I was depending on him to make all the arrangements for our stay. He was simply my friend's brother. And yet, here I was, walking along saying nothing, as if his arrival hadn't made any difference to me, as if it was my right to expect him here to help us out. I felt I must express my happiness, my gratitude. I should speak with him and get to know him a little, create some impression of warmth to make him feel that his arrival at the station was not merely a distasteful duty.

... But was this really Sarla's brother? Sarla and I had been in school together. He'd be twenty-four or twenty-five. Not more than that. Would he be her younger brother? He didn't seem to be. I'd somehow assumed that he would be a mere youngster, maybe fifteen years old or something like that. What if he were somebody else, some kind of a con-man? This sort of thing was quite possible in a big town. At first I'd seen a resemblance with Sarla - but I'd been so thoroughly nervous at that time, that everybody's face seemed to look like Sarla's and her younger brother's! How did he find out that I was waiting for someone...seeing my anxiety perhaps anyone could have guessed it. And I hadn't even waited for him to speak. I'd blurted out, "are you Sarla's younger brother?" But he did ask if I was Kavita. If he wasn't Sarla's brother, how did he know my name? My name wasn't written on any of my baggage was it? I cast a surreptitious glance lest I had put a sticker on any of my bags. I'd actually planned to do that – just as well that I hadn't. Otherwise, I would have worried myself sick that he had read my name form the baggage.

"Sarla had written to you about me?" I asked after considerable hesitation.

"You don't think I'm a magician, do you?" he smiled, "otherwise how would I have known that you were to come by this train and that I was to receive you at the station."

I was tickled and a little vexed too – with him and with myself. After all what was the sense in my question? But then he shouldn't have given this sort of an answer either. Should one talk in this cheeky way with a woman one has only just met? That too, his sister's friend?

He pulled out a letter from his pocket. "Sarla didn't write anything much. Just that her friend Kavita was coming to settle in this city, and that I was to receive her and arrange a place for her to stay."

I relaxed. Nothing to worry about. I hadn't been duped. This was indeed Sarla's brother.

By the time mother and I got there, he had already had the baggage placed in a taxi. While I still fumbled with my handbag, he had paid the *coolie* and sent him off. He had left without a murmur, sure sign that he had received far more than he had expected.

There seemed no point in opening my purse. It was clear from his manner that if I had made an effort to offer the money, he would not have accepted and considering his sharp answer to my earlier question, one could only guess what his response might have been. Piqued, I struggled to close my bag and ended up spoiling the zip. It refused to budge. How I'd begged Ma that she shouldn't insist on buying such a poor quality thing. It wasn't much, but it was wasting money down the drain.

Once the taxi set off, silence descended again, more embarrassing and unsettling than before. At that time we were at least walking. He was busy keeping an eye on the luggage and I concentrated on helping mother. Now we were seated together in the confined space of a taxi. Enough of hesitation and formality. I should ask him a few things, I decided. This would keep the conversation going and I'd pick up some information as well.

I looked at him and sensed that his mind was also working on the same lines and that he was about to ask me something. Somewhat surprised, I stayed silent for a while.

Finally I asked, "where have you arranged for us to stay?"

"In my own house." This was said with such complete naturalness that I could not take his answer as a joke. I couldn't laugh it off. We couldn't possibly stay in their home.

"Wasn't it possible to find some other place?" I had to ask, even though I was reluctant to sound rude.

"Why? You don't want to stay with us?" he asked without looking at me, relapsing into silence as before.

His answer no doubt had the structure of a question, but it was neither a question, nor was he seeking an answer. He had tossed that sentence at me the way we throw a banana peel or any other worthless thing, out of a moving vehicle and then forget about it.

But the question *was* addressed to me even if there was no really correct answer to it.

"No, it's not that." I had to be a little frank, "but you yourself...," I faltered, "as Sarla told me, you stay with your aunt. You don't have your own home here. Of course you'll appreciate it's a little different for you. It would be awkward for me. There's the two of us, Mother and I. I'd hate to be a nuisance." I wanted to see his reaction, then added, " ... and even if one is close, for how long can one stay in another's home?"

After stumbling through all this, I expected an open response. But there was virtually no change in his demeanour.

"No!" The shadow of a smile crossed his face, "you've got me wrong. I have two aunts here. I stay with the elder one and you'll be at the younger one's place. Besides, you'll be staying in her house, not her home."

What a web of words this young fellow was weaving around me, I wondered.

"What does *that* mean?" Perhaps my tone was sharper than I had intended. I added sheepishly, "I don't get it."

"What I meant was, there's an annexe to my aunt's house, a separate portion that she rents out. *That's* where you'll be staying." For the first time, he looked directly at me.

"Then it's okay!"

There wasn't any cause for worry now. This was a perfect arrangement. Sarla's my closest friend. I'll stay now with her family and yet be independent. To live quite alone in an unfamiliar city scared me. This way there would be no cause for fear. They'd give me a feeling of security… but I'd be their tenant. Of course, that is a delicate relationship. Suppose we have the inevitable differences and tensions and I end up losing a friend like Sarla… this new anxiety started weighing me down badly….

The taxi drew up in front of a gate at his instructions. I got off and opening the door, helped mother out. By the time I turned to look, he was bent over the metre checking the fare.

"Let me settle this." I quickly put my hand into my already open purse.

But he'd already paid off the taxi and turned towards the house.

"What have you done!" my eyes filled with disapproval.

"It's alright, it's alright." Like an elder, he patted my back lightly and completely at ease, marched towards the house.

I looked at him, so this was Sarla's younger brother? I'd had a picture in my mind of a mere boy, shy and hesitant, who'd blush when I spoke and look down at his feet. And this! As if he was years older to me. How direct his manner was, familiar and open, as though he had known me for years.

… Could it be that he felt pity for me? Had Sarla mentioned something of that sort. Maybe he was making sure that I didn't spend. But I'd seen Sarla's letter and there wasn't anything like that there. With probing eyes, I tried to gauge. A few steps ahead of us he had stopped and turned around, waiting for us. Sensing my eyes on him, "come," he said and walked ahead.

Entering the gate we walked to the verandah beyond the lawn. An elder lady and a young woman were waiting for us.

This must be Sarla's aunt and her daughter. But I wasn't sure. They could be other tenants. There might be more than one unit rented out. I almost greeted them from a distance but that tenant thing made me desist.

"This is my mausi, my little aunt," he introduced us as we drew near.

I laughed at his words, 'little aunt' and folded my hands in greeting. 'Little' just wasn't the word for this lady – either in age or size. But it didn't seem to upset her. Maybe she didn't understand English… or out of affection, she had given Sarla's brother the license to joke like this.

"And this is my younger sister – little sister or little girl if you like – Sushma. She's a poet." The laughter in his voice was now unmistakable.

I looked at Sushma, young and pretty. Long tapering fingers, delicate hands raised in greeting us and large candid eyes looking at him, brimming with love and vexation all at once.

I responded with a namaste.

"And this is Kavita, Sarla's friend, and this is her mother," he continued introducing us.

There was not a trace of frivolity in his words. Perhaps a sense of the formality of the occasion or maybe it was mother's presence.

"But, do you know who *his highness* is?" She smiled and asked us.

There was no doubt she was going to introduce him in his own special style. I felt somewhat uncertain to how far I should participate in their mutual leg-pulling. How would they feel about my intrusion into their private brother-sister domain. But couldn't a lack of humour or dryness on my part also be offensive?

"I only know that he is Sarla's brother," I said somewhat cautiously, "and that his name is Shailesh."

"Then let me introduce you properly." Sushma looked at him and laughed, "he doesn't know the basics of English. He's utterly blank on this …"

"Come, let's go inside," Mausi said, "you don't have to finish off your quarrel here. Better leave some for indoors as well."

Both Sushma and Shailesh smiled, and bowing in a somewhat courtly style, he asked us to proceed indoors.

So, all of us entered into their drawing-cum-dining room. A large room with a carpet, sofa, centre and side tables. Further ahead was a teak dining table and a large fridge in a corner. The light-coloured walls showed to advantage two large oil paintings, but I couldn't make out what their subject was from afar. Showcases displayed a variety of pretty things and there was an elegant vase to one side with a money plant in it.

When we had set out for this city, I had never imagined a house of this standard nor expected such a warm reception. Sushma and Shailesh's rather unconventional but affectionate manner had succeeded in brushing aside virtually all my misgivings. Still, I felt out of place in this gracious home and was filled with a sense of unease.

It was in an effort to check the rising panic that I asked Sushma as I sat down, "you were saying something?"

Returning to her earlier mood, she said, "Shailesh just doesn't know English. But being a true Indian, he loves to use it. You've heard him yourself translating younger aunt to 'little aunt'. He thinks himself to be another Dr. Johnson and doesn't hesitate at all to generously gift new words to the language!"

"But do give me a full introduction please!" I laughed, claiming for myself the right to join in their affectionate leg-pulling, "you've stopped at his English alone!"

"That's right," smiled Shailesh, "Madam poetess, even if you answer one question perfectly and you leave out all the other questions, you'd still fail. In an exam all your answers should be equally well done. That's my advice."

"Thank you," answered Sushma, then turning to me, "as you know, Shailesh is like his name – the king of mountains. And just like a mountain, his mind is thick and heavy and dull and inactive. Calls himself my 'old brother' which re-translated into Hindi makes 'aged brother'."

"Oh I see!" and I burst out laughing.

Bringing things back to practicalities, Mausi intervened. "I've had your baggage kept in your room and two beds as well. If you'd like to wash up, you could and then have tea to get over the fatigue of the journey." Then looking at the sparring duo, "they're kids, they'll go on like this forever!"

This promptly brought me back to the realities of the present – the journey, the tiredness, our new condition, all had been momentarily forgotten and I should have freshened up long ago. I hadn't even checked before getting down from the train how much dust and grime had got plastered on my face. I wondered how I was looking.

I stood up and looked at Shailesh who, catching my intent, pointed towards the toilet.

Mother followed. I'd forgotten all about her ever since we got off the taxi. In these surroundings, Mother had become a dispensable commodity. What role did she have here? I awoke to the actuality of her presence. I hope she hadn't felt herself to be irrelevant here? That would make things harder for me. Adjusting here would be difficult enough. If Mother's attitudes and reservations got in the way, it would get irksome.

The bathroom was sparkling clean as if everything – taps, shower, flush, basin, mirror – had been polished for us.

"They seem to be nice people," Mother murmured in my ear.

So Mother was happy! I needn't have been so skeptical. She didn't think herself to be unnecessary here. Why had I felt her to be unwanted! Like a being from another planet – a being that had nothing to do with the world of comfort, laughter and fun...

Well, Mother was content! She couldn't bear coldness, formality. Probably, she found warmth in everyone. If she continued to be comfortable like this, then I had nothing to fear as far as she was concerned...

"Ma, I've been telling you from the beginning," I said in a burst of enthusiasm, "Sarla is really a good friend of mine."

"I know that's fine, Kavita." My confidence seemed to erode Mother's sense of wellbeing. Downcast, she confided, "but we're poor. That's why I felt this forbidden happiness..."

"Ma, everything is okay, you just..." Agitated, I walked back towards the room. These sad, upsetting thoughts were hard to accept. Where was the room for sadness in these surroundings? Then why infuse the dismal toxin of gloom here... it was criminal... Sushma and Shailesh's high spirits had given me a magic wand to drive away my despondency. When I saw their good cheer I was no longer conscious of my own problems. Something has begun to change within me, perhaps had already changed... but Mother...

Mausi led us directly to the dining table. Sushma and Shailesh were already seated there. Both of them were silent and their faces suggested that they hadn't been talking before we returned to the room. Perhaps it was others who inspired their witty exchanges.

"Come, please be seated!" Shailesh called out on seeing me.

I sat down.

"Why don't you come this side, *behenji*," Mausi guided Mother. Mother glanced at me smiling, and walking towards

Mausi sat down next to her. With what delicate perception had Mausi realised that the depression that clung to Mother's face would again and again, like some revolting sticky thing, brush against me and raise a tide of anger within me! Subconsciously, I yearned for someone to rid me of the burden of this gloom...A spontaneous flood of warmth, my sincerest gratitude – Mausi aroused these in me with this one simple gesture.

"You're feeling relaxed now?" Shailesh asked me.

His lips were trembling with mischief. Sushma also struggled to control the laughter that threatened to explode. They were definitely planning to let fly some more of their verbal fireworks...

"Excuse me?" What I actually wanted to say was that I didn't know exactly what he meant. If he had given me a chance, I would have asked him to let me come to terms with my new situation, settle down a little. But I feared that his witticisms might unknowingly upset the delicate equilibrium I'd barely achieved and push me back into the world of gloomy hopelessness. I didn't want to be depressed.

"What I meant was..."

"Shailesh!" Mausi had spoken after a long while. "Why don't you talk about something that even an illiterate like me can understand."

So Mausi was illiterate. It could be that when Shailesh called her 'little aunt' she might not have any idea what he was saying. This information gave me a strange sense of assurance. Mausi had money but not education. So there was one area in which she might feel inferior. Mother shouldn't find it at all difficult to interact with her.

Mausi's words hadn't forbidden Shailesh to stop this banter but in effect it served that purpose. She had pleaded her inability to follow their language and Sushma and Shailesh's humour was entirely verbal.

"Listen!" I spoke simply to break my long silence, "you were asking me something."

"Yes, I was." His tone was considerably more sober than before, "I have already told you whatever I know about you, and Sushma is eager to know more. Like, what is your purpose in coming here and things of that sort."

"Sarla hadn't informed you about these things?" I was really amazed.

"Not a thing." He took a sip of tea, "Sarla's your friend so you might not like me telling you, but you don't know her true colours. She's a dictator! You've already seen her letter. There's not a scrap of information in it, only orders."

"Well," I started, "the fact is that I have come to live here permanently. I've just got an appointment in the Girls' High School as a teacher. Sarla and I were classmates. We both did our under graduation together. She went on to do an M.A., I took up a B.Ed. course. I'd already been teaching, but as there was no scope for better pay-scales, I applied here and have been selected. They've sent me the appointment letter and I have only to go now and report to the head mistress with my joining report."

"There's no one else with you?" Sushma asked me directly. Her question was very vague. I think she had already realised that her query could mean virtually anything, so she hastened to explain, "I mean, brothers and sisters, father etc."

"I have one brother, he's younger to me." I was reminded of Satish. How much he bothered about me! He had told me repeatedly when we were leaving, "Didi, let me know as soon as your reach or else I'll keep worrying." And here I was, not once had I thought of him since morning, poor fellow! I continued, "Sushma, he's younger to me in years but in all other things how much older than me he has become!"

In spite of all my efforts, the lightness of mood, the feeling of freedom and calm, all abandoned me and disappeared I don't know where.

"All brothers are like that. Just see that 'mountain' sitting over there," she said looking teasingly at him. "He's much younger than I am. But the way he behaves, anyone would think he's older to me."

"Which class are you in?" I asked, surprised at myself. So preoccupied was I with thoughts of Satish, that I had assumed there was no space for interest or curiosity about any other topic.

"I'm in the M.A. Final and he's in the Previous," she told me, smiling.

"But Satish isn't older only in jest," I said earnestly, myself realising the gravity of my tone, "he'd taken up a job right after completing his tenth standard, and to tell you the truth, has borne the burden of my education since. My father is no longer alive."

"You haven't brought your brother with you?" Shailesh asked.

"He can't give up his job," was my brief reply. I knew how inadequate my answer was, as though I were agitated or something. It was even ill-mannered. To cover up a little, I added, "my pay alone may not have supported the three of us here. Besides, he doesn't want to be dependent on an elder sister whom he has supported so far."

Silence settled over the room. The atmosphere became somber and heavy. No one said a word. What could anyone say after my distressing answer. How could I have known that they would give so much consideration to my troubled spirit. I had better be the one to restore a lighter mood. But what was I to say?

Ultimately, Shailesh spoke.

"Well Mausi, I'd better make a move," and he stood up.

"Sit down Shailesh! What's the hurry." Mausi didn't seem to expect that he would suddenly get up and run off. Surprised, she asked, "You have something important to do?"

Much to my relief, Shailesh's face cleared. His normal spontaneous smile was back and gone were those severe lines.

"No, nothing in particular," he said with a gentle shrug of his shoulders. "But now…"

I knew exactly what he meant by this 'but now '… It was also quite clear that he had no intention of leaving just then. Sarla had sent us to him and he was quite aware of what that responsibility meant. He may have been very close to his aunt, but he must have been aware that it was difficult for us to gauge the degree of his familiarity with her and that we could certainly not impose further on her good nature. There was no way that he could leave us so soon! It was my words that had caused him to get up and run. I was the one who had pushed him with my gloom … do forgive me, Shailesh!

"Listen! Listen!" Sushma caught his arm. "Mountains don't move! Where do you think you're going?"

"Sit down, my dearest boy, do stay!" Mausi said with a definite hint of pleading in her voice!

"Of course I'll sit, Mausi. I'll even have dinner here if you ask me to. But there's one condition." He threw us all into suspense. What was he up to now?

Happily, he had been able to get across the road-block that my dreary talk had created. It hadn't been too hard but he had brought back cheer into the room yet again. I was relieved and determined that I would never say things that would make everyone so silent and force Shailesh to run away.

"Tell me what your condition is and if I can, I'll do my best to satisfy you." Mausi was absolutely delighted and there wasn't a trace of artificiality in her words. “What could be better than fulfilling your wishes. You come here so rarely.”

“Mausi, the condition is,” looking obliquely at Sushma, “tell this ‘little sister’ to begin calling me ‘Shailesh bhaiyya.’ She must give up her rudeness and beg me to stay back for the day!”

“Fat chance!” said Sushma, giving him a hammering on his back, “bhaiyya my foot! *You* can call me Sushma didi. I’m your elder as you know.”

“Then I’m off.” He was already standing. Now he took a couple of steps towards the door.

My heart lurched. He shouldn’t actually go away just when things were shaping well. I wanted him to stay. I would even have asked him to, if it had been proper to speak up in the middle of this squabble. Mother’s eyes also pleaded for him to stay.

Like me she must be thinking of him as our own Shailesh. Mausi and Sushma were still strangers to us. Why was he leaving us so soon and going away? But neither Mother nor I could make him stay. What would I say and what right had I?

“Sushma, why don’t you just go ahead and say it,” Mausi said, “what do you lose anyway and why not indulge your brother. He is the only one you have.”

“Mummy! You always ask me to give in. It’s because he’s my brother, or because he’s younger or because I’m older that I should agree.” Sushma grumbled in the most endearing way.

“How does it matter, my dear,” said Mausi.

“Okay then!” Sushma said, sticking her tongue out at him teasingly. “My dearest Shailesh bhaiyya! We shall be eternally grateful if you stay on with us till evening. I implore you to agree.”

“You’d better beg with folded hands,” Shailesh cribbed.

“Get lost! It’s enough that I’ve said this much,” she squealed.

If Shailesh said anything further she wouldn't plead any more. I held my breath lest these two refused to budge. If Sushma was unrelenting, he might walk off in a huff and it wouldn't really matter very much to them. But I'd suddenly feel insecure.

If only he would look at me, he would understand at once. How desperate I felt at that moment.

But Shailesh did not look this way. He continued to stare at Sushma and she refused to give in.

"Granted! I agree to your pleading." He smiled at last and sat down on his chair.

For the second time since coming here I felt a sudden release of tension. This sense of relief flooding through me seemed to rob me of my ability to say anything meaningful. 'What should I do now' was the question that dodged me repeatedly but I couldn't find an answer. I could sit like this forever, not saying, not doing anything.

At last, with a tremendous effort I spoke, "Mausiji, could you show us the rooms please. I'd like to begin sorting out our things."

"I'll go, Mausiji!" Shailesh stood up before she could answer, "Please come," he said.

There were two small rooms. A tiny verandah in front and a kitchen the size of a rather large cupboard and a few steps to one side, a small bathroom. The entire unit was detached from the main house, a little to the rear, virtually independent. Even the approach was separate, the path leading directly to the front gate. There was very little possibility of interference. Where could I have found a better house… but the rent? How much might that be? Was my joy pre-mature? It wouldn't be proper to ask for any concession and it would be awkward to look for some other flat. Anyway, I really had no appetite for any complications at this stage.

Everything seemed just right. Shailesh had made the perfect choice. How difficult it would have been for me to knock around searching for something suitable. It was so good of Sarla to have helped out like this.

Mausi had sent over two beds. I quickly opened up the bed roll on one of them. Mother was looking utterly spent. The strain of the journey and the stress of an unknown place had taken their toll. Mother had managed till now to hide her tiredness and anxiety, but now her energy had run out, or perhaps, alone here she no longer felt it necessary to maintain a façade. She had become absolutely lifeless. Poor Mother! I made her lie down and she did so without protest.

Shailesh and I went to the other room.

"Please!" he began, "I feel that sometimes people don't understand me or else misunderstand me. Must be something to do with my, stars I suppose," he laughed. "If a situation requires me to speak frankly, you won't have a problem with that I hope?"

"No, what problem?" I smiled. What was he going to ask me? At that moment I suddenly remembered.

"Please do sit down for a moment." I shifted one of the two old cane chairs lying in the room. Had Mausi kept them there for our use or had an earlier tenant abandoned them there? When I had left home, Sarla had given me a letter addressed to Shailesh. I'd forgotten all about it in the excitement of our arrival. I now fetched it from my trunk.

Opening the envelope he began to read and as long as he read the letter, I tried to read his face. I had no idea what Sarla had written but while reading, Shailesh looked far different from the young fellow full of pranks and wisecracks of a short while ago.

Even as he pushed the letter back into its envelope, the old Shailesh had already reappeared. Laughing, he said, "I was uselessly blaming Sarla. She has told me everything about you in this. And you know, she's written one very interesting thing." He laughed out loud with undisguised delight. "Do you know what?

"What?" Startled, I looked at him. There was a smile on my face but inside my head I was furiously wondering, what was this 'interesting' thing?

"She's written, you're completely new to this city, you're absolutely alone as you don't know a soul here. So, till you're here I've been appointed your local guardian." He paused, "is that arrangement okay with you?"

"What problem can I have with that!" I was half joking but I meant it too. "If someone is ready to take my problems on his shoulders and becomes my bodyguard as well, why would I complain?"

I'd barely spoken and the thought flashed through my mind that he might say, "if that's the case, why don't you get married?"

But he said no such thing. Could be the playful segment of his mind hadn't worked in that direction or maybe he felt improper to make a joke of my obvious weaknesses.

He got completely into the practical mode.

"That's it then!" he said. "If you are not too tired, why don't you unpack your things. We'll put them away and go out for lunch."

"Where'll we go?" I asked.

"To Mausi's," he laughed, "where else! Would you prefer a restaurant?"

"No! There's no need to go out for lunch," I said "but we won't go to Mausi's either. We've given her enough trouble already. I'll manage this." And, for fear that he might give a clever twist to my words, I immediately added, "as their tenants, for how long can we take advantage of their goodness?"

"No, no!" His tone was both agitated and pleading, he said, "you are our guests today. From tomorrow, we'll let you free! Then you can get your kitchen going."

I didn't protest.

In truth, I wasn't in the mood to say anything, and after all, I could have protested only if I hadn't liked what he was saying. What a load of doubts and fears I'd brought with me! And here was this wonderful welcome! Who wouldn't have loved it? Besides, it would be wonderful to avoid the nuisance of cooking today after the tiring journey.

We unpacked the boxes and arranged the things as best as we could. There wasn't too much stuff, and no fancy things at all. Just the necessities that only required to be stacked away. No pictures or show pieces that could have needed planning or aesthetic skills. Yes, there were some books which would have to be arranged properly later.

Shailesh helped me do all this. He had quite literally, made himself my guardian. He kept up a steady stream of advice which I quietly went on obeying. A complete surrender, the pliant feminine disposition surrendering without resistance to the male will! I don't ever remember having accepted orders thus by virtue of male superiority, or for that matter, of following them so gladly.

"Why are you so quiet? Why don't you say something," he said, turning towards me, "don't you think that staying silent only deepens one's gloom?"

As he said this, I could make out that he became progressively more serious, "If you ask me, the root cause of our country's ill-health is that, we don't speak out our minds. It has lost the gift of speech, because it has abandoned its own language and become dumb."

Right or wrong, I was in no mood at this time to think about or discuss our country's sickness and health, or the language problem for that matter! I would have preferred to know more about him and tell him about myself and try creating a bond with him.

"You know what I think?" I said, sitting down upon the empty trunk.

"Mausi didn't ask you to stay back so that you abandon her and go around helping me with the unpacking."

"As far as Mausi is concerned," he laughed, "it's enough for her that I'm around. Anywhere in her compound... besides, there's nothing more to do here, so we can as well go across right away."

"Yes, Mausi is really very fond of you." I was fully aware that this was not something that he didn't know too well.

"Quite right, I even feel sometimes that she loves me more than she does Sushma. The fact is, that among my mother and two mausis – they're three sisters – I'm the only son. You get the picture, the only brother in the midst of all my sisters. So you see, I'm actually quite the favourite!"

"Oh!" I looked at him, impressed and just a little envious, "how lucky you are! All the sisters doting on you, lavishing their attention on you." I was left wondering if it was only the love of his sisters that he received?

"But then, I alone have also to help each one of them out with whatever she wants," he remarked laughing loudly. "Being the only brother of five sisters is fraught with innumerable dangers. It's not easy. Every one of my sisters wields her full authority over me."

The unpacking was done. And everything was more or less in place. Just then Sushma came to call us.

"Please come, lunch is ready," she said with great warmth and taking hold of my elbow as one would with an old friend, she helped me get up. "Where's Aunty?"

"She's lying down in the next room," I told her.

"Could she be asleep?" she said, almost to herself, "then we shouldn't wake her up, she maybe quite tired."

But Mother was awake. She didn't find it all that easy to get to sleep. She got up to go for lunch without fuss, though to disagree with others or impose her will was not in Mother's nature at all.

Once we had finished lunch, Mausi persuaded us to stay. She was conscious that Mother was tired and had already arranged for her to rest there. Sometimes it seemed to me that Mausi's attentiveness and eagerness that we stay had something to do with her fear that Shailesh might leave if we did.

We had our evening tea with them and Shailesh stayed on. The conversation moved easily from formal to serious, to the familiar banter between Sushma and Shailesh. Off and on, in the midst of the conversation, Shailesh continued to give me bits and pieces of information and advice. Where my school was, what would be the best way to get there, what I should say to my head mistress and the changes I would need to make to adjust to life in an unknown city. He had really taken upon himself full responsibility for all my needs and seemed determined to do a perfect job. Could he be doing all this for me only because I was Sarla's friend? Would just a letter from Sarla have made such a deep impression on him? Would he behave like this with anyone who arrived with a letter from her? It had to be his innate nature.

In the end, I couldn't stop myself. Taking shelter behind laughter I blurted out, "you've taken all my problems upon your head. I'm afraid you might even have to do the teaching at school for me!"

This didn't ruffle him. He said earnestly, "The fact is, you've been sent by Sarla. If you're put to the slightest inconvenience, she'll kill me. She's a very tough taskmaster. Her name may mean 'simple' but she is far from being simple. A regular slave-driver is what she is, who knows exactly how to get her work done." Laughing, he added, "Sushma calls her, Empress Sarla."

"Liar!" Sushma protested.

"And suppose I tell Sarla all you've been saying?" I said to tease him.

"No problem," he said, smiling sweetly to show me how unperturbed he was by my threat, "she'll forgive this 'little brother' of hers."

When he got up to leave in the evening, he tutored Sushma, "You just look after them." Then turning towards me, "don't worry. My 'little sister' is actually a wonderful person, very affectionate, very considerate. Please tell her if you need anything. Tomorrow, by evening, I'll try to look in, if I can. Right, off I go then…bye."

Sushma and I raised our hands in farewell.

When I lay down at night, film-like, the events of the day rolled before my eyes. How smoothly everything had fallen into place whereas my mind had been riddled with fears of all kinds. Shailesh had received us at the station. He had recognised me, and all his arrangements were perfect. Shailesh and Sarla - a tide of gratitude washed over me. Truly, it was Sarla who had given me the courage to come here. She had laughed at all the reasons I had given her why I shouldn't go to a new place. Her words still ring in my ears, "Kavita, don't you worry. My weird little brother is studying there. He lives with my mausi and has been there for many years. He'll fix everything."

Her calling him 'weird' had really amused me then: But no other adjective could have summed up his personality so well. He really was weird. He was extremely close to Mausi and Sushma and had his own equation with them. He could act as he pleased with them, without hesitation. But, was it proper for him to have behaved in this frivolous way in front of us, on the very first day? As though he hadn't thought of us as strangers, as guests at all – neither of these, not for a single moment. He embraced us as his own, and put at rest every misgiving that we might have had.

Satish's face came before me next. And here were we, another pair, a brother and sister who had never had the time for any of these things. It had never even occurred to us that siblings could share such a relationship. Poor Satish! What hadn't he had to do in this brief life of his! Father passed away when he was doing his tenth. He had appeared for his exams during this period of severe stress and, at the age of seventeen; life's heavy yoke had been placed across his shoulders, robbing him of his youth. He had managed somehow to make sure that I completed my under-graduation, but was it really a younger brother's job to do this, when he was himself hardly more than a boy? He had done this and much more. Like an elder brother, like a father, he had become an umbrella over me, to shelter me from all my troubles, and be the head of our family. He had become my protector, when in reality this little brother of mine, had every right to put his head on my lap, and demand love and encouragement. Not once had he asked me for anything for himself. How could I call myself his older sister? Surely seniority comes from giving, not merely from years.

I felt thoroughly depressed.

If only Satish could have come here with us!

How I wished!

When we were considering my new job, this was a major

dilemma. Mother could either stay with Satish so that she could look after him, or come with me here to provide at least a nominal show of protection. To save from the curiosity and gossip that an unmarried daughter alone in a big city, was likely to arouse.

Poor Mother, she could stay either here or there!

Finally, Mother had come with me. Despite my being older than Satish, I was deemed the weaker. So for the same reason would Shailesh have to put up with me, just as Satish had done? But why should Shailesh? Satish had borne it all because that was the hand that fate had dealt him. Shailesh, on the other hand, was the much-loved brother of five joyous sisters. I had no right whatsoever to rob him of his happiness. No, never would I let Sarla or her brother suffer because of me. My gloomy shadow must not darken their lives. No, never!

Next, my school came to my mind. What would it be like – *my* school, but to me still strange and unfamiliar. What kind of person would the head mistress be? The students? My colleagues? Panic was now waiting to grip me.

Next day, I went to school.

Shailesh had thought of everything. He had discussed the route in such detail that like a seasoned commuter, I settled the fare with the auto driver, and guided him confidently to the school gate.

The head mistress had not yet arrived but the attendant told me that by 10 o'clock, she would definitely be there. I went and introduced myself to the head clerk who made be sit down while the attendant opened the head mistress's room so that I could see her as soon as she arrived.

Miss Sengupta gave me not only a most affectionate welcome, but also spoke very frankly with me. She went as far as to admit that she had wanted a local teacher whom she knew very well for this post, but since the selection was not in her hands, I had been appointed by the education department. She hastened to assure me that she had no problem with this and that she looked forward to an extremely cordial relationship with me.

I really couldn't have expected a more open discussion. In broken sentences I tried to convey my feelings to her. I would not give her any opportunity for disappointment with me, either as a teacher or as a human being. As I spoke, I was aware that I had become quite emotional, my voice was trembling and gratitude had made my eyes moist.

On a sheet of paper taken from her desk, I wrote my joining report and handed it to her. She read it, and when she raised her eyes, it seemed to me that they were full of affection for me.

"That's fine," she said, "your work for today is over. Tomorrow please come and take charge. You'll find everything ready and can meet your students as well."

Some hidden power made me fold my hands and take leave.

She smiled and I left her room.

I came home feeling quite buoyant. I calculated that to get the household functioning, dozens of odds and ends would be needed. Shailesh was to come over in the evening, and as there was no point in delay, I'd ask him to come with me to the market so that I could get whatever was required.

The thought of Shailesh gave me an additional boost. For the first time, I admitted how much pleasure his conversation gave me. Just one day with him and he had already become so dear to me. Sarla's 'weird' brother was at this stage my first and only support in this city. If he had been a dry, boring person there was nothing I could have done about it. It was such a blessing that he was weird! My spirits soared.

At home, Mother was sitting near the door waiting for me.

"Mother, why are you sitting out here? Why aren't you resting? Have you got over yesterday's tiredness?" I asked.

I had asked Mother a string of questions but I was seeking no answers. They were but the outpouring of my elated, cheerful mind. Somewhere deep down in my heart, I wished that Mother would say that there wasn't a trace of tiredness anymore and that she was now at peace.

But those feelings that I craved to see did not appear on her face.

"There's naturally some tiredness," she said wearily. "But there's also loneliness. I don't know a single person around here. After you left for school, I came and sat at the door and I've only been waiting for you since then." Her voice turned sadder than before, "I'm missing Satish! I wonder how he's managing there by himself. What if he doesn't eat properly or goes hungry?"

I tried not to give too much importance to Mother's dispirited mood. It was clear even to her that I couldn't be sitting with her all day. I had to go to school. But I didn't allow any annoyance to sharpen my tone.

"But I'm home early today Mother!" I told her, "from tomorrow, it will be evening by the time I come."

"All right, we'll see how things go." Stiff with sitting there, she placed her hands on her knees and getting up painfully, made her way into the room.

Standing in the middle of the room I looked around. Everything we had carried with us had been given a place. Now we had to see how to make it look better. Anyone looking at the room should be able to discern not only order but some traces of aesthetics well…

But then, there awoke within me what I could call my personal critic, a voice that addressed me, "who will see? For whom is the room being made pretty?"

From time to time, this critic present inside me wakes up, and with knife in hand, asks me such questions. He peels away, layer by layer, every trace of hypocrisy, untruth, deceit from my personality.

Before this watchdog I acknowledged without any hesitation that it was indeed Shailesh for whom I had wanted to make the house presentable. I wanted him to admire the room when he came, and approve my taste.

What would I serve him when he came? There was nothing at home and I had no idea whether there was a shop or restaurant nearby from where I could get something. I yearned to do a hundred things, I made fancy plans, but always found myself unable to translate them into reality.

Shailesh came at 5 o'clock in the evening.

"What happened at school?" he asked without a preamble.

"What could happen!" I laughed, "You had prepared me so perfectly, I got there without any bother at all and I am back safe and sound."

"But what did you do there?" he asked.

"I've given my joining report."

"You didn't teach?"

"I'll start from tomorrow."

"And what madam, will you teach?" he asked, looking at me with a look of complete innocence.

"What rubbish you're talking!" I blurted out without thinking. Coming from him the word 'madam' sounded silly to me, but I really shouldn't have spoken to him like that. I certainly didn't want to give him the impression that I did not know how to enjoy a joke or that he didn't have the right to joke with me. Now *I* was the one feeling silly.

"Please sit," and I hastily left the room.

In the kitchen I made some tea and came back in a jiffy.

"Hey! What's this you're doing?" he said

"Why, won't you have a cup of tea in our home?" I asked.

"No, nothing like that at all," he replied in all seriousness, "but why get into these formalities."

"It's only a cup of tea," I said, "I would feel quite rotten if you didn't have it."

"All right." He picked up the cup, "so you're feeling more settled now, not bothered or anything?"

He was smiling.

"Everything is fine. There's no sign of tension is there? But…" I stopped.

"Forget it, no nothing." Why had I let myself even think that I would take him along with me to the market. I felt a bit foolish. I'd begun to think and act as though instead of being Sarla's brother, he was my friend, someone with whom I could be having an affair.

"Do tell me!" he persisted, "don't hesitate."

"I needed to pick up a few things," I said most reluctantly, "from tomorrow I may not get the time, so I thought if I could get out with you today. I could do some shopping and get to know the market as well. Then I can go on my own next time."

"Yes, sure, why not!" He quickly finished his tea.

I had made his coming with me into such a big issue. He had accepted it most naturally without any sign of excitement or stress, rather as though he was about to launch out on some novel enterprise. I was struck by my own childishness, while I felt a new sense of respect for his good sense.

We set off soon.

"Please, where…"

He stopped me in my tracks, "this kind of formality just won't do. Why don't you call my by my name?"

I was well aware that in comparison to how close I felt to him, my way of addressing him was far too distant. But quite honestly, there had been no occasion so far to shed formality.

"I've no problem with that. I'll call you by name," I said, "no more formal behaviour anymore."

To remove distances and become more familiar, one has to climb so many little stairs. Perhaps addressing by name is the final stair. After that, one is free to climb other steps as the relationship demands. But surely, permission has to be taken before venturing on to this final step...

... And that was when my personal critic awoke again.

Where am I heading? Is it only the barriers of formality are being removed? Did I truly have no other wish or desire in mind? I stood my ground firmly, unwavering. "No, there's nothing else." It was my personal guardian who backed off. "Right, there's nothing." But he warned me, even as he left, "nevertheless, be careful."

We went around a bit aimlessly, from one shop to the next, without any particular thing in mind. We roamed more than we shopped, but he showed me around the bazaar so that I could find my way around alone and avoid being cheated. This ramble through the market was accompanied by a running commentary about his University. Embellished with endless anecdotes and jokes, Shailesh gave me a thoroughly entertaining account of his activities in college, the peculiarities of his professors, who resembled whom, who taught well, which one was scholarly and who was merely filling a slot, like a joker in a pack of cards.

Later, when I went over all these things, I was left wandering what it was that had made his narration so amusing. I had laughed helplessly. Those who had seen me at that time must surely have thought me to be mad. Totally unaware, this had not struck me then. When one is so tickled, who can be bothered with such silly concerns!

He dropped me off at home, but avoided coming in, even though I asked him to.

"Well, I'd better be off," he said, "I'll spend a little time with my 'little aunt' and 'little sister' before I go."

"Shailesh, thank you so much!" I said earnestly, "I've given you a lot of trouble."

He glared at me. "Sssh!" tapping me gently on my head as he moved off.

For a long time afterwards, my hand went back to stroke that part of my head. His behaviour didn't seem at all unnatural. In fact, it would have been quite out of character if he hadn't made some gesture or the other of this kind. These were the whimsical features of his personality. How could anyone take offence?

It was a pity that everyone in school was not like Miss Sengupta! So, whereas the head mistress was no problem at all, equations were not so simple among the teachers. Either they were overwhelmingly curious or completely indifferent. When they eyed me with interest, I felt like a new arrival in the zoo. On the other hand, when there was overt disregard, it was as though I didn't exist at all.

I hadn't really expected to be welcomed with open arms, nor hoped to become one of them straight away. But neither had I thought that there would be these old friendships and alliances, which like an impenetrable wall, would never let me in and shut me out forever. Within each group, most of them knew each other so thoroughly that their husbands were friends, their children played together and they met for outings. I had no such contacts to offer. There were no shared experiences that would bind us together or spontaneously draw us closer.

It was all very correct and formal. When there was a meeting, I could simply sit there quietly, since everyone had only to sit and listen to those who spoke. If there was some specific work to be done, personal or official, a question about the timetable for example, or where I could buy reasonably priced stationery, I would address them in my politest voice, with either a 'Miss' or a 'Mrs' appended to their name. But, nothing beyond that.

One day, I reached school quite early. So early that the attendant hadn't unlocked the staff-room. The door was quickly unlocked and a chair dusted for me. He threw open the windows and asked if he could get me anything.

"No Girdhari, thank you."

It was most awkward to sit alone like this. I may not have any friends as yet, but it isn't as if I wouldn't talk to anyone. I felt like cursing myself for getting here so early!

Just at that moment, Rima and Jyotsna walked into the staff-room together. They may have bumped into each other here at the gate, or perhaps they were in the habit of setting off together from home. I had no idea. Anyhow, they had arrived and it would probably be easier for me to seek their friendship rather than that of anyone else's.

They seemed surprised to see me sitting there. They may not have expected anyone to be there before them.

"Hello Kavita!" Rima said, as soon as she saw me, "here so early..." looking clearly taken aback.

Somehow, her look of amazement made me feel good. If it had been any of the senior teachers they would have ignored me as if I weren't in the room at all. Not only did Rima notice me, she actually looked at me; she even recognised me, greeting me by name.

"Yes, I got here much too early today," I said, "I really miscalculated."

"We've also come a little early," Jyotsna said.

If I'm not mistaken, it was the first time I had heard her voice. I too speak softly, but compared to the way Jyotsna spoke, I sounded shrill. She made me feel, I don't know why, as if she were much better, far superior to me.

Rima appeared to have read my expression well. "Jyotsna speaks very softly," she explained.

"I'd never noticed before," I replied.

"That's why you didn't find out." It was Jyotsna who spoke up, "that's what the teachers have against me. They complain that I'm whispering things about them all the time and that's why I speak so low. And here I can't understand why everyone speaks so loudly!"

From that day on my friendship with them grew steadily. In fact we soon became a separate group in ourselves. There was no longer any need to cultivate anyone else. We purposely stayed together as much as we could, ignoring everyone else. During recess, we'd sit by ourselves, leave for home at the same time when school was over and definitely meet briefly between periods.

My association with Rima and Jyotsna made one thing clear to me. The other teachers made no effort to befriend me, but they had nothing against me. But as for Rima and Jyotsna, they were undoubtedly hostile to these two over some issues. Jyotsna's habit of speaking so softly had made matters worse. The general grouse was that she was perpetually speaking ill of them. If this wasn't true, why didn't she speak normally like everyone else did?

But these two were quite happy to be on their own and cared very little for others. I'd tell myself every once in a while, that the friendship or hostility of others hardly mattered. I had no quarrel at all with anyone, but there was no denying that before these two befriended me, I'd been pretty much like an orphan in the school. So now, if because of my friendship with Rima and Jyotsna, the others began to dislike me as well, how could it really hurt me...

I must admit though that I didn't always feel this sure of myself. At times I'd be very dejected. How could I cope with the ill will of everyone in the staff except for these two? When the others, looked at me at me with disapproving eyes, I crumbled from within. I began to feel suffocated. At such moments I felt like running away somewhere, but where?

Without doubt, this collective hostility had succeeded in taking a complete hold of my imagination. The minute I left home, my thoughts were exclusively caught up with these issues. So completely in fact, that I virtually lost awareness of my own personal predicaments. I would try to forget my habitual anxieties, about the staff or my home, in the thrill of what had become something of an addiction...

And because of this external pressure on our friendship, Rima, Jyotsna and I began to draw closer in, all our activities, even those outside school. We had begun to crave each others' company well beyond the contact at school. We would set out together wherever we wanted to go. Trips to the market, roaming about, outings to the cinema, we would not go without one another.

In their company, my confidence soared and there was a drastic increase in my going out. In the past I had put off buying even essentials, till it became almost impossible to manage, because I so much disliked going to the bazaar alone. And now to buy even a pencil, the three of us would go together and make a regular expedition of it, entering a dozen shops for the smallest thing. We began to eat out or go to the cinema more and more often, things I had rarely done before. Naturally, all this began to tell on my expenses.

All this dawned on me one day while shopping. I had bought

myself a pretty pink sari from the Silk Emporium and selected a pair of sandals to match. When I looked in my handbag, I discovered to my horror that there was no money. There was nothing at home or in the bank because I knew I had been roaming around with all the cash in my bag. All I had was about twenty-five rupees, whereas the sandals themselves cost thirty and there were still five more days till the end of the month...

"I'll come again." Telling the shopkeeper I got up urging Rima and Jyotsna to follow me out.

Puzzled, they left the shop.

"What happened, Kavita?" Rima asked, "you had selected the sandals and then didn't take them. And then you ran as if there was a mad dog after you."

"I didn't have the money," I said in a small voice.

"You could have taken the money from me," Jyotsna said, "where was the need to leave those sandals!"

"No. I'll buy them next month," I said.

"By then they'll be gone," Rima warned, "and without matching shoes how will you wear that sari to school tomorrow.'

"Never mind," I stalled.

I was truly worried and angry. Angry with myself. What was I doing! Where was I heading? Why don't I keep in mind the reality? How can I forget our condition...?

At home, when Ma saw the sari, she muttered, "yes, it's nice," and then added, "but you buy so many things for yourself, why not send something for your brother sometimes?"

I had no idea what untold depths of bitterness were hidden within me. Like burning lava it came flowing out at Mother's words, "why not a new sari for you!"

My own tone left me stunned. What was wrong with me! What was I saying and to whom. To Mother who refused to take medicines simply to avoid spending my money. To Mother, who had left her saint-like son Satish so that I could have a job here, even though there was no arrangement at all for Satish's meals.

But Mother, my dear innocent Mother, probably missed the sarcasm of my words or deliberately ignored it. She said in the same simple way, "Well, this sari is all worn out but I'm all right..."

That brought me to my senses. To my utter disgrace, Mother's sari *was* torn. Was I blind. My Mother didn't have decent clothes to wear and for myself I needed silk saris and matching footwear...

For a long time I lay on my bed and cried. Again and again, I asked myself what was wrong with me, what had I become, why was I untrue to myself? Why had I forgotten my mother, my brother. For me, they had made every conceivable sacrifice and now I could no longer see that my mother's clothes were shabby. And when in simple good faith she asked me to send something for my brother, I scourged her with my stinging words. Never had my brother ever demanded anything from me. He had given me much, taken nothing. And I...

It was, as if, in these last few months, I had been living in a dream. It had been a life of fun and laughter, films and restaurants, saris and shoes. No trace of poverty or sorrow, depression or anxiety, nothing at all...couldn't my mother, couldn't my brother give me this sort of life? Was it possible that they were my enemies. In a peculiar way, I began to dread them.

But how *could* I have forgotten them? Not one of them had I remembered, neither Mother, nor Satish, nor Shailesh! Shailesh! Why haven't you come for such a long time!

I couldn't myself understand what it was that I really wanted. If Mother and Satish were dear to me then why can't I let Rima and Jyotsna go? But if I need them, then why can't I forget Mother and Satish? And Sailesh…after all, what do I really want?

Soon after, Rima and Jyotsna toyed with the idea of seeing a film. Did I want to go or not, I kept asking myself. Unable to make up my mind, I gave them neither a clear 'yes' nor a definite 'no'. The result was, they bought a ticket for me and I had no choice but to go.

Entangled in the web of my own confused thoughts, I could hardly concentrate on the film. Innumerable times, I reminded myself that having spent the money, I might as well watch the film, and the thoughts could be sorted out later. But nothing worked. I would focus for a while but then my mind would wander off again. It was hopeless!

Maybe it was because my mind was so distracted, that I became extra conscious of Rima and Jyotsna sitting next to me. It struck me that they were more interested in talking to each other than in watching the film. They would look at the screen for a while, but soon enough they'd look at each other and begin to smile, or else bending close, talk softly together. I continued to look at them but I couldn't catch a word of what they were saying.

Then, in a flash, the thought crossed my mind. Were they talking about me?

I couldn't contain myself.

"Rima, what's up?" I asked.

She turned and looked at me. I could make out a faint smile on her face in the darkness of the hall. Then she turned back towards Jyotsna.

"Do tell me. What is it?" I insisted pinching her arm.

She swerved instantly, "nothing sweetie! You watch the film."

So they were brushing me off, hiding something from me. I

had lulled myself into thinking that they were my friends, that I was one of them, but they were double-crossing me. This could only mean that I'd been a fool. I was not one of them, I was an outsider, an intruder.

I was separate. There were things that they didn't want to share with me. Who knows, it could even be that these were things about me. May be they had ganged up against me.

In the hall I could not persist, so I remained silent. But inside I was boiling, ashamed of my stupidity and furious at their meanness. No wonder everyone in school felt the way they did about them. When the three of us sat in the corner of the staff room, murmuring among ourselves, refusing to say anything much when asked, how rotten the others must have felt, how dreadful we must have looked...

In this agitated state it was difficult to keep sitting there. I felt like getting up and going home. But something held me back. If I left, they could carry on talking as they pleased which I had no intention of letting them do at this moment. Besides, I'd have to be very clear about one thing before I provoked them. There wasn't a single other person in the school whom I could call my friend. When I had chosen to join these two, I had knowingly shut the door on all the others. Now if I alienated this pair...

Finally, the film was over. Silently I got up, and without saying a word, walked out in front of them. My expression was completely normal, but they had certainly changed.

"Why Kavita!" Rima asked, clutching me by my shoulders, "you're very quiet. Are you cross with us?"

"How can I be cross with you? What right do I have?" I said indignantly. "You two just carry on murmuring to each other. When I ask you what's happening, you don't tell me anything and ask me to watch the film!"

"What my dearest Kavita, so this has upset you!" she said sweetly, "you're much too cruel!"

I was taken aback. There was no regret in her voice. It didn't seem at all as if she felt she had done anything wrong or that any explanation was going to be offered.

"Why?" I asked.

"Okay, you tell me. Would it be possible to talk loudly in the cinema hall? There were so many people sitting next to us. You know that we'd have told you afterwards," she said, turning the tables on me.

"But what was it anyway?" I couldn't help asking.

"I was only telling Jyotsna," Rima said, "that just as the nurse in the movie had seduced the doctor, she should use the same tactics on her Rakesh and catch him!"

"What?" I asked flabbergasted, "who's this Rakesh, Jyotsna?"

"She hasn't told you," Rima said feigning ignorance, "she's rotten! He's a lecturer in the University. She's ready to die for him and he doesn't care for her."

"So you're advising seduction, are you!" I had no idea where my anger had vanished, as I joined in the banter.

"What else!" Rima said with a martyred air, "if honesty doesn't work on some people one has to find other means, isn't it?"

"Why don't *you* capture him then?" I said, moving from banter to clowning.

"Don't you worry about her!" Jyotsna spoke a little louder than normal. "This clever female has got her eyes on the National Store fellow! She helps herself to whatever she fancies and the poor fool doesn't even ask her for money, tries to please her instead."

"What?" this too was news to me, totally unexpected. I just stood there and gaped.

"And you, Kavita?" Now Jyotsna was smiling.

"Me? Don't be silly…!" I could myself hear the sadness in my tone, "where's the space for romance in this broken heart of mine?"

"Poor girl!" Rima remarked pityingly.

"Why don't you try," Jyotsna urged, "I'm scared of my brothers. They'd murder me if they saw me with anybody. What's your problem, you don't have a soul here."

"Never!" I said faltering, as though I'd been asked to commit a heinous crime, "I'd never do a thing like that."

One evening Shailesh came over.

"Hello Kavita, how are you?"

Immediately my spirits lifted. It seemed to me that losing myself in all sorts of trivialities, I had purposely pushed him somewhere far from my circle of consciousness. But now, when he was standing right there before me in flesh and blood, I could no longer deceive myself, nor could I hide the truth from him.

"Well! Fine!" I said, swept along on a surge of excitement "How come? I thought you'd forgotten that you're supposed to be my local guardian here. It's been ages since you came," I complained even though I hadn't wanted to.

"Yes, I don't come," he nodded, "but remember, your slippers are still at Bata's for repair?"

What *was* this fellow saying! The same old unpredictable statements! What on earth had my slippers got to do with his not coming, and *which* slippers, anyway?

Puzzled, I said, "I don't get it."

"People choose *not* to understand things of this sort," he said, abandoning his sober tone, "especially if there's nothing to be gained by it. What I was saying was this, I agree that I haven't come here in a long time, but all the trips that you've made to my place must naturally have worn out your slippers, and by now, they would be lying for repair at Bata."

Guffawing with delight, I burst out laughing. The same familiar stupid conversation! But what a mild smartly- cloaked complaint!

"Me?" I asked innocently, "But I'm already living in your house... I'm sitting right where you had dumped me, waiting patiently for you to come..."

And as if from nowhere, the critic from within asked me. "Is there any sense in what I had said?"

Recollecting the answer I had given to Shailesh, I was left flustered, bewildered, not fully comprehending what was going on...

In my embarrassment, I fell back upon formalities, "but seriously, how is everything?"

"How am I? Bad! Just very bad indeed!" He seemed serious but was he? He laughed, "the exams are coming by special express delivery. You folks have all the fun. No need to think or study, just stroll across to the school when you feel like, pull up the kids for something or the other, shout and scold a bit, and then come strolling right back home again."

"Okay, okay!" I laughed. "Where's the need to scold the poor brats. Is there any harm in just coming back home? If you had to bellow for a full six periods, then you'd know just what strolling to school and strolling right back again means!"

"In other words, you are just as miserable too?" he asked.

"What do you think?" I smiled.

"Where is the need for me to know?" He turned serious all of a sudden. "Full two thousand years ago a man called Buddha has left us with no choice. He told us that the world is a valley of sorrow. Every human being is unhappy. Birth itself is the root cause of sorrow…" then, his mood altering again, "let's forget it and go out for a while."

So it was a mix of exams and the Buddha that had brought him here. But at least he does think of me, feels the need to meet me, I felt.

"Just sit down a moment, I'll ask Mother and come," I said and went into the other room.

Asking Mother was only an excuse. Of course I would tell her, but I wanted the time to change quickly and give my hair a brisk comb.

Mother's face fell. She didn't like my going. But why? Was Mother still bothered by loneliness? Now that I stayed away for hours together, she must be used to it. Or could it be that she was missing Satish? It was Mother's lack of cheer at moments such as this that was becoming intolerable to me these days. The minute I felt happy or relaxed, Mother's low spirits would douse the flames of my enthusiasm as effectively as a shower of icy water would have done. Then I would be completely put off… and Mother was gradually being transformed into some sort of a bugbear for me. It felt as though I was beginning to avoid Mother and dread her responses.

"What is it Mother?" I asked.

Mother looked at me in a way that asked me whether I shouldn't myself understand what she meant. Then softly she said, "It isn't very proper for you to go out so often with a young man."

I found it difficult to decide whether I should laugh or cry. What does Mother think! Am I a thoughtless little child or is Shailesh some unknown stranger? She knew quite well that this is our Sarla's younger brother, Mausi's precious nephew and Sushma's beloved brother. Why does Mother worry so much!

"Ma, this is not any young man," I laughed and tried to bring the matter to a lighter perspective, "this is Shailesh, Shailesh!"

"It doesn't matter who it is," Ma's tone didn't change at all, "we're poor and people gossip about us more readily. No one raises a finger at the rich that easily."

Mother's views were very antiquated. I'd ignored them several times in the past. Why did our poverty stick like a leech to Mother's consciousness? Our lack of resources bothered me too, but purely as a handicap of a practical nature.

Ignoring mother, I went out with Shailesh. I didn't want him to find out what we had talked about, nor give him the slightest hint that he had been the topic of discussion in the other room. But my mood had been completely ruined and I couldn't hide it. I tried hard, but Shailesh understood all right.

"What happened Kavita? Was mother objecting?" he asked.

So he did know! It was no use protesting. I wouldn't have been able to cover up.

"Yes," I acknowledged.

"But why on earth are you upset with me?" He was looking straight in my eye. "I'm pretty sure that I haven't been rude or stupid enough to have taken any liberty with her majesty and annoyed her?"

"Where am I cross with you," I was unable to laugh at his witticism. This was something more serious and I couldn't get over it so easily. "It's mother's ways I'm so wretched about. She manages to find something negative in everything."

His joking had failed to raise my spirits but my solemnity refused to dampen him.

"But it's for your own good." I suspect his remark was meant to tease me, provoke me.

"My own good, my foot!" I was acutely aware that she was my mother. Any differences between us were our own business. Speaking of our problems before an outsider, complaining about her wasn't correct. I'd been waiting for so long, for the right person to whom I could speak frankly about these things to ease my mind. But there was this huge conflict. I wanted to but felt I shouldn't, I was trying to restrain myself but I was talking out as well. "Mother's always been like this, but now she's much worse. Irritable, ready to cry at every little thing."

"But why," he asked, "there's got to be a reason."

"What reason will there be?" I said, steadily worked up. "Worries all the time about my marriage. Harping on it day and night. If I'm not getting married what can *I* do about it!"

The watch-dog within me spoke up at once: was I deliberately raising this topic, was I trying to give him some sort of hint…

This frightened me. I quickly changed the subject... "And then, all the time mother thinks about Satish. Sometimes it's really bad: the poor fellow must be alone, how does he manage his food, who takes care of him? Along with this, add her one-point agenda - marriage, and things get totally out of hand." I stopped mid track.

"And what else," I suppose he still hoped to hear much more.

"Let's forget about this." By now I was much calmer and dearly wanted to drop this subject. "You must be cursing that I've gone on about my dreary sob-story. It's bad enough that I'm so thoroughly disheartened by endless discouragement, but why burden you as well?"

"Kavita, you've got me all wrong." Here he was, standing in front of me. Sarla's strange little kid brother stripped of all pretence.

Every layer of outward appearance peeled away to reveal himself as he truly was. He was clearly tired of this outer self being mistaken as his full reality. He seemed to want me to know that inner self. "There's little else that we can do for one another, except share our little sorrows," he said, "It's another matter if you don't wish to tell me. I can't compel you to lay bare your thoughts but believe me, one is always honoured by someone's trust"

I was completely won over! Such hidden depths in this young man whom I had refused to take seriously. What compassion and capacity for love! He wanted me to open my heart to him, share my innermost thoughts, my doubts and fears, my joys and sorrows!

This was an offer of friendship. Could I ask for more?

"No, there's nothing to hide. And certainly not from you, Shailesh!" I was overcome, my mind freed of restraint, freshened by some external fountain of energy and strength. "Mother is troubled 24 hours by a single thought, we are poor. So what should I do? Have we no right to live if we're poor? When you do anything, buy anything, go out anywhere, feel happy or good, there's only one refrain, 'we're poor', 'we're' poor'!"

My sudden outburst didn't shake him at all. He was there, as calm and firm as he had been before. Not a shadow of anger or irritation crossed his face. He understood what I was saying. "It's not her fault Kavita! It's possible that in today's world we aren't able to fathom her state of mind. Maybe, we can't understand because these are not our experiences. The experiences we have, the course that our lives take teach us to think and feel the way we do. She's probably been conditioned by the age-old values that poverty is a sign of inferiority, that it is a punishment for past sins. At her age there's no way that she can change her attitude. So there's just no point in getting upset."

I stood there wonder-struck. Could this be the same Shailesh!

I said nothing further. He too was busy with his own thoughts. Silently we walked along, and I had no desire to disturb this silence.

"I'm feeling terribly hungry," Shailesh said all of a sudden. "Is there any problem with eating out once in a while? Everyday we eat at home in any case."

Before I could have answered 'yes' or 'no', we had already walked into a restaurant.

Only once in the past had I been out with Shailesh to the market. That was right at the beginning when I had been a complete stranger whom no one recognised. I had felt no hesitation then, but today I was haunted by the fear of being seen sitting there with Shailesh.

Shailesh gestured towards a table and I quietly sat down.

"Now then, what will you have?" he asked, his eyes scanning the menu.

"You're forgetting," I smiled, " it's you who's hungry, not me. I had something with my evening tea."

"Okay, then you can sit and admire."

He called the waiter and ordered a plate of cheese sandwiches and some coffee.

We ate and we chatted but he didn't eat as though he was really hungry or anything.

Most of the time he asked me questions about my school, the kind of people there, my routine. These were the main topics. Whether he was merely being polite or he really wanted to know, I couldn't make out. Nevertheless, I told him everything. What sort of person Miss Sengupta was, how the other teachers were and about Rima and Jyotsna, my friendship with them and how we were seen as a group of our own.

So there he was, sitting in front of me in his role as my guardian. What I told him sounded to me, less like answers to specific questions, and more like a report card of my activities. And at the end, the same question, "there aren't any problems are there?" And every time, when I'd nod my head and say 'no' he would be satisfied.

We finally made a plan to go for a film. An excellent movie was showing in the matinee and the next day was a Sunday. I was very keen that he come home in the morning itself, we could all have tea together, and then leave for the cinema. But there was no way that he would agree. He insisted that I go to his house and that we get out for the film from there. Ultimately, I had to give in. If he had been ready to listen it would have been different but seeing that he was adamant, I really had no choice.

Shailesh saw me home.

"Thank you," I said before going in.

"Don't be funny," and playfully patting me on the head, he left.

Feeling light, walking on air, I went indoors, but Mother's tone dragged me down from a world of dreams and stood me squarely on the ground without delay.

"There's a letter from Satish in the evening post," she was saying.

A letter from Satish! I got a jolt. It looked as if, casting away my old world, I was trying to soar to forbidden heights, but clutching at my hand, reality was wrenching me back so that it could fling me back into my own universe once again. Satish's letter must have brought with it the familiar air of gloom. He must have written about his problems. Every time that's what happens.

I was truly put off. Why did he have to talk about those things that reminded me again and again that he had sacrificed everything for my sake; that it's for the sake of my happiness alone, that he was putting up single-handedly with everything there. And here, Mother never let me forget that only because of me she had to endure loneliness. What is it that these two wanted from me?

The very next moment, my own inner critic, rebuked me roundly: "What sort of a sister am I! Instead of being excited at getting news of my brother, I've flared up. If he does convey his sense of deprivation, why does it upset me so much? Why do I want to deny the truth? He *has* lost much because of me, has shared my problems and taken them upon himself. This is the truth I should face. That's the reality. I am the reason why others have to suffer..."

I opened his letter and read it through in a single go. He had already warned us that he felt shaky about his job. It was after all, a temporary one. He wrote now, that it was more or less certain that he would lose his job any day. He had differences with his boss, and was wondering whether he should leave his present job and join us in the city to try and find a better opening there? He felt that since he was in any case getting older, it would probably be wise to try and make a fresh beginning, which could in the future, become a permanent place for him...

Was he crazy! Give up his job and come here? Did he have any idea how expensive these big cities were. It was hard enough for the two of us to manage on my salary, and if he came to! What was the sense in chucking up his job because his boss was unhappy with him. Had he made an effort to work hard. And talk of his getting older and the need to settle in life? Was he suggesting that he wanted to marry?

I was afraid I would scream. Satish! My younger brother, planning his marriage.

Couldn't he see that I, his elder sister, was still around unmarried. Hadn't he realised that finding a suitable match and getting me married was also his responsibility. Why didn't he think about my marriage instead?

I was frantic, but only for a passing moment. Before I knew, the critic in me was asking me if I indeed wanted to marry at all? If I do indeed wish to marry why don't I do something about it myself, the way Rima and Jyotsna were thinking. Or, why don't I tell Mother to think about it. Why do I presume that Satish should do everything for me. And, if he does succeed in finding a partner, would I accept his choice and marry?

I steadily fell in my own esteem. How base, how selfish I was! Never had I given my younger brother anything, had always been taking from him. Now for the first time, when he'd expressed a desire for something, I was concerned only with satisfying my own need.

I felt like throwing myself on the bed, and crying my heart out into my pillow. But Mother was right there, waiting anxiously for me to tell her what Satish had written.

The next morning I reached Shailesh's house. He introduced me to his 'old aunty' and also his 'tiny sister', Seema. His behaviour with this aunt was a great deal more formal, while his love for Seema was there for all to see. So different from his way with Sushma. She was more than his equal in anything one might care to name. So their usual exchange took the form of a battle of wits, a friendly trial of strength. Seema was much younger and so there was no attempt to equal him at all. Rather, like a devoted little puppy, she followed him about. It was, 'bhaiyya' this and 'bhaiyya' that! For her he was clearly an elder and but for nurturing affection, what else could he have given her?

I do not know why, but the thought hiding in the recesses of my mind was that Shailesh would not have spoken to anyone about our plan to see a film. He could introduce me at home as Sarla's friend, but what was the logic for going to a film with me. Besides, the family didn't always know what boys were up to, where they went, whom they met. I was therefore surprised to learn that everyone at home knew about the programme and Seema was hugely excited about going with us.

Seema's going with us had somehow put me off. I wasn't able to fully comprehend my strange reaction. The excitement, the enthusiasm subsided and yet, I felt relieved as well, as though I had been saved from some grave peril. Now I was safe. I would not come to harm and I would not cause harm to anyone. That's how I felt.

The booking-window was open by the time we reached. There wasn't much of a crowd so there was no chance of our having to return home disappointed. Seema and I positioned ourselves against a wall, away from the queue and waited, while Shailesh went for the tickets.

"Didi! Didi! Look," she pointed to the posters, isn't this one pretty!"

Both of us were busy scanning these.

"Kavita!"

I turned around. There were Rima and Jyotsna.

"Hi!" Delighted, I eagerly went forward, "you folks too..."

But unlike me, neither of them seemed pleased nor did they make any move to come towards me. They stood at a distance smiling at me in a dry sort of way.

What's the matter, I wondered.

"You're a smart one, putting us on like this!" Jyotsna said, her lips distorting a little more than usual. "Not me! Not me! Indeed!"

I was taken aback. What did they want to know? Why these daggers in their eyes and snide smiles on their lips?

"What do you mean?" I asked.

"Don't you be too smart with us!" Rima thumped me on the shoulder. Her behaviour in this public place seemed coarse and artificial. "Who is he?"

"Who, this Shailesh?" I asked as light began to dawn on me.

"What do I know if it's Shailesh or Ramesh," Rima smiled again.

"Have you got your tickets or may I get them for you?" Shailesh asked.

"No, we've bought the tickets, thanks," Jyotsna smiled and spoke in her carefully cultivated soft voice.

"Okay then!" Rima turned.

Shailesh greeted them with folded hands and stood aside and I too moved back a little to let them pass.

As she passed, Rima, seeming to say good-bye, whispered in my ear, "fine fish you've caught, but he's a little underage, isn't he?"

By the time I could raise my head, turn and look at her, they'd both gone.

I was dazed. What had I heard! What was this she had said!

"Didi! Come!" Shailesh was already close to the door while Seema was tugging at my hand. In that one instant I felt that the old Kavita had died. Life seemed to have been drained from me and I was dragged along by Seema like a lifeless thing.

"Good fish you've caught", "have caught … good fish … have caught". My mind was in a spin, like I was wandering in some old abandoned ruins, with ghosts and spirits shrieking in my ears. Voices, loud and soft, echoing everywhere. My eyes closed in terror and I was just a pair of ears. But these ears could hear none of the sounds from the screen in front of me. Could not follow what Seema was asking, nor what Shailesh might have said. Only the numerous goblins howling in my ears. "Ha, ha, ha! … have caught …. good fish …. have caught!"

Rima had seduced the fellow from the National Store. She bought free stuff from his shop, in return for giving him false smiles. She was playing around with him, deceiving him. I too have trapped Shailesh. He's young, immature. He doesn't understand. I'm the cunning one, older to him, who has ensnared him, taking unfair advantage of his innocence, his inexperience. He's the doting young man, I the adult heroine in this sordid drama. I have trapped and deceived Shailesh who is Sarla's brother. Not of Sarla alone but also brother to Sushma and Seema. Sarla, my Sarla, dearest friend who has helped me whenever I have been troubled… who has been like a ray of hope in my life. The Sarla who trusted me, sent me to Shailesh, she handed Shailesh over to me, or rather handed me over to Shailesh. And now I am cheating this Shailesh, who has shared my tears and sorrows and given me nothing but happiness. I am betraying this very same Shailesh, trapping and stealing him from Sarla, Sushma, Seema, badi Mausi and choti Mausi, from all of them.

No, this should never happen. I am indebted to Sarla and beholden to Shailesh. I love Sushma and Seema and cannot be false to them. I cannot ensnare this fun-loving young man! I will not let them, any of them get hurt in any way. The bleak shadow of my own life will not darken their golden world. Sarla, I won't cause you any misery, I will not take from you your brother. Never…

"Kavita! What are you thinking?" Shailesh touched my shoulder to rouse me from my reverie, "It's the interval."

"What are you thinking?" he asked again, "what's happened

to you? This is only a movie. You can be pretty sure the hero and heroine will be united soon enough. You're far too sensitive."

"Yes, I do get a bit carried away," I said to cover my embarrassment.

"Didi, shall we go out?" Seema asked.

"No, Seema, I'm okay here," I said, "Sailesh, why don't you get her an ice-cream or something!" "Come, let's go, Chutki!"

I quickly fished in my bag for some money but he had already taken Seema out.

I couldn't concentrate even after the interval. All I wanted was to get away from this place, run away from it all. Go to a place so far that none should be able to say that I was after Shailesh or that I had my trapped him. I could not cheat Sarla who has given me unflinching support. I will not betray her trust. I must not meet Shailesh again, not ever again.

The film was over. We flowed along with the crowd that streamed out of the hall. I was painfully aware of Shailesh's gaze on me. He wanted to say something I think, but was unable to. And I no longer trusted myself enough to ask him what it was he wanted to say.

"I'm sorry Kavita!" Shailesh finally said, "if I had known you get so sentimental, I would never have brought you to a film of this kind."

Flustered, I laughed an embarrassed, apologetic sort of laugh but stayed silent. I wonder what he had made of my laugh. After that, not much was said on the way home. He asked me a couple of casual questions which I handled with a simple 'yes' or 'no'. Gauging my mood, he wanted to leave me alone. That's what I thought.

When Shailesh and Seema turned to bid me good-bye at the door, I didn't even ask them to come in. Raising my hand in farewell, I smiled politely, and they left. For a time, I continued to look at his retreating back, asking myself, "am I really deceiving him?"

When she saw me, Mother asked if something was the matter, but I evaded any further questioning by telling her the film was far too heavy and it had spoiled my mood. Mother did her best to encourage me not to take things to heart, and finally left me with the advice that I should stay away from such movies in the future...

My thoughts turned to a fresh line of argument. Could it be that I had been taken in far too easily by these two devils and accepted that I was indeed guilty. In what way was I trapping Shailesh? He himself came over whenever he felt like. He had taken me to the market, had insisted we go to a restaurant and it was his idea that we go to a film. He was himself drawing closer to me. Where is it that I had done wrong?

Why on earth didn't I say 'no' to him. Why didn't I convince him that too much familiarity with me was not at all in his interest? Why didn't I try to turn him towards the right path? Why didn't I tell him that our lives just didn't match, that there was far too much difference between his world and mine? That any day, he would most definitely, get an infinitely better, younger, prettier girl than me.

But once I had told him all this, would I be able to live without seeing him? Would I be able to manage without him? And what about him, wouldn't he like to continue meeting me.... But these bonds had to be broken. I must face it. No matter how miserable I felt I had to stay away from Shailesh.

Next day at school when I met Rima, she asked, "Who was he?"

And Jyotsna, "Who was he?"

"He's my landlady's nephew," I answered matte-of-factly.

"Wonderful!" exclaimed Rima, "you have really caught a big fish."

"You won't have to pay any rent," Jyotsna suggested.

"Then why don't you capture some house owner yourself?" I said, annoyed.

"Not everyone is that lucky!" sighed Jyotsna.

"A home is a huge thing, dearie!" Rima said, chucking me under the chin, "here's my fellow unwilling to give me even a sari. 'Father will be upset' he says to pacify me. It's just that your stars are extra special."

I was deeply hurt by their disgustingly loose talk. I had barely got over the previous day's taunt and now this. They refuse to be put off, these horrid women, maligning me without any cause. They think everyone is as vulgar as they are.

My conscience-keeper was standing there before me. "Are you sure that you don't have any relationship with Shailesh? Not even attraction?" "There is nothing at all. It is only friendship, pure and simple!" He was not convinced. He glared at me pointedly, "nothing but friendship? Not even attraction?" I could look him in the eye. I conceded, "there is, there is, there is. Of course there is!"

My mind was thrown into a bitter struggle. What is it? Why is it? What have I done wrong, Shailesh comes because of his own wish...Does he? Have I not encouraged him. Forget encouraged, I've actually attracted him... I've done it, yes, definitely. Rima is perfectly right! I'm the one to blame... I'm the culprit. I am cheating Sarla, cheating Shailesh as well...

For a week I met no one, neither Shailesh, nor Sushma, nor Seema and nor Mausi.

But one evening, Sushma came over.

"What's the matter, Kavita?" she asked as soon as she came in, "you haven't had any differences with Shailesh, have you?"

"No, why?" startled, I protested, "who told you this." "No one's said anything," she said, "but it seemed so to me."

"No, not at all. Where's the question of a fight." I needed to explain myself, "just last Sunday Shailesh, Seema and I went together to see a film. After that we haven't met." I looked at her, "What made you think so?"

"He's been here since morning," Sushma told me, "when I asked him to come across and look you up, he ignored the suggestion. When I asked a second time, I thought he would hammer me!"

"But why?" I couldn't understand what was going on, "nothing like that at all. Sushma, you must be mistaken!"

"Then come," she said pulling me up by my arm, "you come and find out for yourself."

'Should I go', was the big question in my mind.

That question mark soon became a lethal sword hanging over my head. Should I go? Should I go?

A sharp cry rang out and continued to echo and re- echo, striking again and again the walls of my mind. It continued to echo, like lightning that strikes the tallest peak of a mountain, and then wanders through the valley from one corner to the other, 'don't go! Don't go Kavita, don't go! This is the perfect opportunity, he has himself begun to loosen the bonds, cut the ties. This is the best opportunity you will ever get. Don't go.'

Will I never meet Shailesh again? There was a tight knot in my stomach – an agonising ache. My lips went dry and my head reeled.

The sound of 'don't go, don't go' echoing through my head, I set off with Sushma.

And there sat Shailesh, morose and glum. When I entered, he gave no indication whatsoever that I had come in or that he had in any way registered my presence. What I truly wanted to do, was to run and sit down, kneeling in front of him and turning his face towards me with my hand, ask him what was after all the matter.

But I checked myself. If I had let go even the slightest bit my mind would have run riot and then there'd have been no controlling myself.

"What's happened to you dear little sulky child?" I said, trying to sound playful.

"Don't you talk to me," and putting on a grumpy face, he turned the other way.

"Say something to me," I pleaded in a most restrained manner, "at least give me a reason. I don't think I've said or done anything to upset you."

"That's right! You haven't done a thing. It's just that I'm crazy," grimacing, he looked at me.

"The day we went to the film you said you would come to my place," he shot back, "then you didn't come nor did you send any message."

"I had said I would come?" surprised, I was more or less asking myself, "I don't remember a thing."

"Then I'm lying??" he grumbled petulantly like a child.

What could I say? I didn't remember a thing. I was hardly myself that day.

"Okay, I made a mistake," I said trying to make light of it, "I'm sorry."

"Then friends again?" he asked, like a child who had got his mother to yield to his wishes.

"Sure!" I was charmed by his innocence.

"But one condition."

"What?"

"Tomorrow you'll come to my place."

"Tomorrow." I was unable to say the word 'no'.

My eyes were fixed on him. How to refuse him? How to break off with one who, like a child, gets so easily upset at the slightest thing and is ready to make up again in a jiffy.

"All right, I'll try."

"Not try," he ordered, "you have to come."

"Okay, okay, I'll come." A voice was chiming within me, 'I'll come! I'll come!' And instantly my watchdog stood smiling in one corner, 'that's all the determination you have, is it!'

"Good." He stood up.

"That's done," so far silent, Sushma teased, "put off like a baby and as readily made up. And then you boast that you are my elder brother!"

"Quiet!" and giving her a gentle push on her back he went off to his 'little aunty'.

All night I couldn't sleep.

I have to take some clear decision. I can't leave him forever on uncertain ground, nor can my mind stay in a perpetual dilemma. Tomorrow if I do not go, he would be unhappy with me and perhaps he would never see me again. If I do go, our intimacy would surely grow. He will come closer. I would become weaker and more desperate in his presence, and he more familiar. Then, it is possible, he might come to have new expectations of me, and I wouldn't be able to refuse…

When he is in front of me I melt, become weak. I feel overwhelmed…. No, I'll go. He's so like a child. He isn't capable of discriminating, of choosing between what's good for him and what's not.... Then I have to be the one to act sensibly. I shouldn't meet him...shouldn't meet him...

The whole of the next day passed in this indecision. I went to school but was not myself. I did the work somehow, mechanically. The bells rang and the time passed. I returned home in a daze. I expected to hear a knock on the door, I would open it, and see Shailesh standing there, waiting for my apology. Or Sushma would be waiting to tell me again, how Shailesh was cross with me.

I would turn to the door again and again, but no one came. Every ray of the setting sun beckoned me and left, but I did not get up, I did not move. The golden sun too grew dim, and darkness lay upon everything. But none was there to call me.

Then a tidal wave surged within me. Wave upon wave of words, urgently climbing one over the other, 'I'll go, I'll go, I'll have to go.'

And beating against these, 'don't go! Don't go!'

Clutching my head with both my hands I lay face down upon my bed.

Next morning Sushma came to call me. Shailesh was waiting on the phone for me.

The receiver in my hand trembled, "hello."

"Kavita," it was Shailesh's voice, "remember your promise!"

"Yes, I remember, Shailesh."

"I'm not going to listen to a thing," his stubborn tone took on a distinct edge, "are you coming today or not?"

The firmness of his tone scared me. And like before, I became helpless. A hundred voices rang out, "I'll come, Shailesh, I'll come!"

"Hey, word of honour?"

"Yes Shailesh, I'll come."

"Okay," and he disconnected the phone.

Then I came to my senses. What have I done! Why can't I refuse him? To promise and then not go, it would be better to refuse outright. At least he wouldn't think I was a liar. Why can't I tell him truthfully, Shailesh, my world is a separate one, my mother and Satish and I. I was wrong to think that we can leave that world behind and step into your world, the world of Sarla, Sushma and Seema. I cannot free myself of my world. I cannot be part of any other world, not yours, nor Rima's nor Jyotsna's. Let me be, Shailesh! I don't have the courage… but to turn away from Shailesh, to reject him thus?

This day too passed like the day before. Each moment played itself out once more. Wave upon wave of resolve rose again to a crescendo, and the bells of denial echoed and re-echoed once again. I sat there clutching my head. The sun sank steadily to its rest. Each setting ray beckoned to me till its final departure. Then there was no one left to order me, to summon me, to beckon me. The darkness deepened and I continued to sit….

FULL CIRCLE publishes books on inspirational subjects, religion, philosophy, and natural health. The objective is to help make an attitudinal shift towards a more peaceful, loving, non-combative, non-threatening, compassionate and healing world.

FULL CIRCLE continues its commitment towards creating a peaceful and harmonious world and towards rekindling the joyous, divine nature of the human spirit.

Our fine books are available at all leading bookstores across the country.

FULL CIRCLE *PUBLISHING*

Editorial Office

J-40, Jorbagh Lane, New Delhi-110003
Tel: 24620063, 24621011 • Fax: 24645795
E-mail: fullcircle@vsnl.com • website: www.atfullcircle.com

Bookstores

5B, Khan Market, New Delhi-110003
Tel: 24655641/2/3

N-8, Greater Kailash Part I Market, New Delhi-110048
Tel: 29245641/3/4

Number 8, Nizamuddin East Market, New Delhi-110013
Tel: 41826124, 41826125

Yes, I would like to be a member of the

World Wisdom Book Club

Name ☐ Mr ☐ Mrs ☐ Ms..

Mailing Address..

....

....

City.................................. Pin.......................................

Phone.................................. Fax....................................

E-mail..

Profession............................. D.O.B.............................

Areas of Interest...

....

Mail this form to:

The World Wisdom Book Club

J-40, Jorbagh Lane, New Delhi-110003
Tel: 24620063, 24621011 • Fax: 24645795